SUSAN COOPER is a world-renowned author
of children's books. Born and brought up in
England, she worked as a journalist before
moving to America, where she now lives. Her
classic The Dark Is Rising sequence has won
the Newbery Medal and was twice shortlisted
for the Carnegie Medal. Her Boggart titles
have won the Scottish Arts Council Children's
Book Award and been shortlisted for the
Carnegie Medal and the Smarties Prize. *King
of Shadows* was also shortlisted for the
Carnegie Medal. As well as writing novels,
Susan Cooper has written for the theatre and
for television.

You can find out more about Susan Cooper
on her website www.thelostland.com and
follow her on Facebook www.facebook.com/
SusanCooperFanPage

Books by Susan Cooper

THE BOGGART
THE BOGGART AND THE MONSTER
THE BOGGART FIGHTS BACK

OVER SEA, UNDER STONE
THE DARK IS RISING
GREENWITCH
THE GREY KING
SILVER ON THE TREE
THE DARK IS RISING SEQUENCE
(A collection of all five books)

DAWN OF FEAR
KING OF SHADOWS
GHOST HAWK

SUSAN COOPER

The BOGGART

A PUFFIN BOOK

PUFFIN BOOKS

UK | USA | Canada | Ireland | Australia
India | New Zealand | South Africa

Puffin Books is part of the Penguin Random House group of companies
whose addresses can be found at global.penguinrandomhouse.com.

www.penguin.co.uk
www.puffin.co.uk
www.ladybird.co.uk

First published by The Bodley Head Children's Books 1993
Published in Puffin Books 1994
This edition published 2018

001

Text copyright © Susan Cooper, 1993

The moral right of the author has been asserted

Set in 12.5/16.5 pt Sabon LT Std
Typeset by Jouve (UK), Milton Keynes
Printed in Great Britain by Clays Ltd, St Ives plc

A CIP catalogue record for this book is available from the British Library

ISBN: 978-0-241-32681-7

All correspondence to:
Puffin Books
Penguin Random House Children's
80 Strand, London WC2R ORL

MIX
Paper from
responsible sources
FSC® C018179

Penguin Random House is committed to a
sustainable future for our business, our readers
and our planet. This book is made from Forest
Stewardship Council® certified paper.

in memory of
BILL
1946–1986

with love

Author's Note

In writing this book I have borrowed certain real places and shamelessly altered them. Castle Keep and the Camerons' store bear only a glancing resemblance to Castle Stalker and the excellent village grocery shop in Port Appin, Argyll, and their occupants are fictional. So are the members of the company of the Chervil Playhouse, which is an echo of the Tarragon Theatre in Toronto. Most of what I know about writing for the theatre I learned from the late Urjo Kareda, artistic director of the Tarragon, but Robert Volnik is not Urjo. The Chervil's dog, however, was real. At the Tarragon they called her Clio.

I am grateful to the late Charles Dunn for the Boggart's Gaelic, to my friends the Campbells, the Karedas and Catherine Ashmore for their help in Toronto, and to my son Jonathan, Michael Weishan and Pete Magsig for their advice on computers.

CHAPTER ONE

THE LITTLE boat crept closer, over the grey-green water of the loch. Tommy could hear the slow creaking of the rowlocks, and see the white hair of the lean old man bent over the oars. His father said the MacDevon was one hundred years old, but Tommy had never had the courage to ask if it were true. The MacDevon was a clan chief, the last of his line, and you didn't ask a clan chief a question like that.

'Good day, Mr MacDevon.' He caught the bow of the dinghy as it crunched into the small stones of the beach. This was a weekly ritual: the old man's shopping trip from the island of Castle Keep.

'Aye,' said the MacDevon, in his soft, rusty voice.

'Have you not brought Fergus?' Tommy was astonished; the old man never went anywhere without his dog.

'Fergus is old and tired, Thomas. Like his master.' The MacDevon stepped over the side of the dinghy, lifting his big rubber boots as if they were too heavy for him. Out of the boat he took a deep shopping basket woven of wicker, grey-brown with age. Then he walked carefully up the beach towards the village store, in which Tommy's mother struggled to fill all at once the jobs of grocer, bookseller, fruiterer, postmistress and occasionally – if Tommy went fishing – fishmonger. She used her son as delivery boy, though he preferred the fishing.

Tommy tugged the dinghy further up the beach and looked out over the water to the MacDevon's island. It was no more than a rock, really: a grass-skinned slab from which the square grey bulk of Castle Keep rose like a box of stone. The castle's grey sides were streaked yellow with lichen; there were only a few windows, and those cut so small, against attack from long-ago invaders or the everlasting Highland wind, that the walls seemed blind. It was a small castle, as castles go, but it was handsome and forbidding there alone in the loch, with the water all around and the hills of Mull rising misty beyond. Though Tommy rowed over to the island now and again, to deliver groceries or mail, he had seldom been inside. Nor had anyone else from the village. The days were long gone when Castle Keep rang with the revelling of clansmen gathered from all over the Western Isles, and every neighbour strained to hear the haunting music of the great piper MacCrimmon of Skye. Now the castle stood silent and empty, and the last MacDevon lived there alone with Fergus his dog.

But not quite alone.

Tommy gasped, jumping suddenly backwards, as a strand of wet seaweed was flipped up into his face from something in the bottom of the empty boat. He thought: *So you're here again this time, are you?* For an instant he heard the thread of a laugh, from the thing in the boat that he could not see. A very ancient, mischievous thing, solitary and sly, born of a magic as old as the rocks and the waves. A thing that had lived in Castle Keep for all the centuries of the MacDevon clan, and longer.

The Boggart had come shopping too.

Tommy's mother weighed out the apples, and put them in the MacDevon's basket. She frowned at the keys of her cash register, as she carefully punched in the prices of apples, bread, oatmeal, milk, and so she failed to see one of the apples rise quickly into the air and float sideways. But Tommy saw. Instinctively he put out a hand and snatched the apple as it passed, and from somewhere in the air he heard the echo of a small resentful wail. He handed the apple to the MacDevon. A smile flickered over the MacDevon's pleated brown face, and he winked at Tommy with one of his bright eyes as he put the apple back in the basket with the rest. Nearby, the air seemed to quiver for a moment, as if something swiftly passed.

'So, Mrs Cameron,' said the MacDevon, 'is there any mail for me?'

'No, Mr MacDevon, not this week,' said Tommy's mother, as she said every week.

'Well now – what is the news?' he said.

Mrs Cameron paused to think. She was a pretty woman, but looked always slightly worried, perhaps by the fecklessness of Tommy's father, Angus Cameron, who as usual was away somewhere chasing a story. He was the Argyll correspondent for several Glasgow and London newspapers. By the standards of Glasgow and London, not much news was made in Argyll.

She said, 'Mrs MacNeil's youngest, Sue, has had twins in Aberdeen.'

Tommy said eagerly, 'And my father has a great new computer.'

'Ah,' said the MacDevon, without interest. In the course of his very long life he had resisted nearly all change; there was not even electricity in Castle Keep.

Mrs Cameron sighed. 'There it sits in its box waiting for Angus,' she said. 'And whether he will be able to talk to it I very much doubt.'

'I can help him,' Tommy said confidently.

'I'm sure you could,' said his mother, without much hope, 'if he will just stay in the one place long enough.'

Suddenly Tommy heard a bicycle bell ringing from outside the shop door, where six bicycles bought by his optimistic father stood waiting in a patient row for athletic tourists to come and rent them. He ran hopefully outside – and was greeted instantly by a great jangling crash as all six bicycles tumbled into a heap.

Tommy stood staring. Nobody was there. And he had not touched any of the bicycles, not one.

Mrs Cameron called crossly '*Tommy!* What are you *doing*?'

From the other side of the bicycles, in a triumphant whisper of sound, the Boggart laughed.

Swinging his golden tail, Fergus lumbered to his feet, as the MacDevon opened the great door into the castle's draughty hall. Fergus was an elderly Labrador, deaf and almost blind, and all his world now was focused on the presence and smell and touch of the MacDevon. His master rubbed his head absently, and moved towards the kitchen, carrying his basket. With his fine new packet of oatmeal from the Camerons' shop, he had a mind to make a nice warming bowl of porridge for his tea.

Behind him, the Boggart swiftly transformed himself into a large hairy brown spider, and danced provocatively on the tip of Fergus' hot dry nose. Once, this would have produced gratifyingly hysterical howls and barks. But Fergus was too blind to see the spider; he only sneezed, and shook his head, sending the Boggart rolling head over his eight heels on the floor.

It was the Boggart's turn to sneeze, in the dust that lay thick all through Castle Keep. He changed back into his own shapeless invisible self, and flickered away to sulk on a windowsill. Outside, a fine soft rain began to fall, and all the surrounding coasts of the Western Highlands of Scotland and the Island of Mull disappeared into the mist.

For more centuries than he could count, the Boggart had lived at the edge of whatever family of MacDevons inhabited Castle Keep. He had no idea where he had come from. Nor did they. Sometimes the family knew he was there, sometimes there was nobody who noticed – though this offended the Boggart's pride, and usually he would put the situation to rights by behaviour so outrageous that even the most earthbound human would sense that magic was at work. (Once, in the sixteenth century, in the time of a particularly bone-headed MacDevon, he had had to leave a grinning luminous skull suspended in mid-air over the castle steps for a full week before the clan chief stopped, looked up, and shrieked.)

The present MacDevon, last of his line, had known about the Boggart since the day when he lay in his cradle and heard something invisible squeaking like a mouse in his ear. Instead of crying, he had laughed. It was the first laugh of his life. Thus he had grown up to become a man who enjoyed practical jokes even when he himself was the object of them, and he and the Boggart had lived in silent mutual appreciation ever since.

The Boggart was his own master. Being one of the Old Things of the world, he was not made for human warmth; he belonged to the cold separate heart of the Wild Magic, which like everything that is wild operates by the law of the survival of the fittest. He did no hurt to anyone, but he lived for the satisfaction of teasing and trickery, and if the humans around him objected to his jokes they would find those jokes taking on a quality very close to malice. A boggart, by his nature, feels warmth for no one.

But once, in the faraway past, the Boggart of Castle Keep had broken this rule. Once, perhaps as much as a thousand years ago, there had been a chieftain of the MacDevon clan called Duncan, whom the Boggart had loved. This chieftain too had recognized the Boggart from his cradle, and smiled at his escapades, and through all the years of their friendship the Boggart had happily played his tricks on Duncan, and Duncan had laughed. But then, in one of the battles that bloodied the Highlands often in those years, Duncan MacDevon was killed, by a blow from the sword of an invading Norseman. And the Boggart had lost his friend.

All the members of the MacDevon clan gathered, after the murder of Duncan, and they took his body over the water to the Island of Mull. In procession they carried him, sadly, the whole length of the island, through the bare purple-green mountains and through the rocky passes. They went on foot, hundreds of them, in a long file, for days, with a single muffled drum beating before the body of Duncan and a single piper playing his bagpipe behind. There was an irregular creaking all the way, from the wooden wheels of the cart which bore the coffin. The piper's lament paused sometimes, since pipers need breath, but the slow rhythmic beat of the drum never stopped.

All along the track called the Road of the Chiefs they took Duncan MacDevon, through the mist and rain, until they came to the far coast of Mull, where in a little fleet of boats and coracles they crossed the water to the holy island of Columcille, which is also called Iona. The drum beat still as they carried their dead chief over the sea, and the pipe wailed its lament. And on Iona they buried him in the ground of Reilig Odhrain, the quiet graveyard where for centuries Scotsmen have laid the bodies of saints and abbots and clan chieftains, and more than sixty kings.

And all the way from Castle Keep to the island of Iona the Boggart went unseen with the procession, staying close to the body of Duncan, weeping. After the clansmen went home he stayed for a long time on Iona, listening to the gulls wailing in the sky like the lament of the bagpipe, and watching while the grass grew on Duncan's grave. When the grave was green he went back to the castle, and for twenty years he lay quiet and made no sound or movement, nor played any trick on anybody. By the end of the twenty years he had forgotten why he was grieving, since he was a boggart and not a man, and he began to play tricks on the MacDevon clan once more. But once in a great while he remembered that he had felt pain, a terrible ache in his heart, and he swore he would never let himself feel love for a human again.

The Boggart flittered away from the windowsill. Thinking about his successful trick with the bicycles, his revenge on Tommy for rescuing the flying apple, he felt cheerful and sprightly, ready to find a heap of new ways to turn the MacDevon's life upside down. He went to his own private place in the castle, a space between two blocks of stone high in a wall of the library, where three hundred years earlier an absent-minded mason had forgotten to put mortar, and an absent-minded carpenter had hidden the forgetfulness with a shelf. There he stayed, plotting and gleefully planning, while the MacDevon scraped the remains of his porridge into Fergus' dish, to replace the dog food that gave such trouble to the poor old dog's few remaining teeth.

The MacDevon felt very weary, suddenly; too weary even to go to bed. He sat down in his big armchair beside the fire, and Fergus, licking the porridge off his nose, flopped down with his chin over his master's feet. Through a mist of fatigue the MacDevon thought of the Boggart, and wished he had put out an apple for him in some obvious ridiculous place, like the bath. Then he remembered that he had left all the apples he had bought in a bowl on the kitchen table, and that the Boggart loved to steal one or two things from any bowl, to leave him perplexed about how many had been there. It was the thought of the Boggart enjoying his stolen apple which brought an affectionate smile to the MacDevon's mouth, a smile which was still there when he fell asleep.

Next morning a pale ray of sunshine slanted in through the library window, glanced up off a glass inkwell on an old desk, and woke the Boggart in his cubbyhole high in the wall. He basked in the light for a while, happily contemplating the day ahead. There was not much fun in playing tricks on Fergus any more, since the old dog scarcely noticed anything but the touch of the MacDevon's hand on his head. But the MacDevon still took obvious pleasure in any piece of teasing – the more ingenious the better. And his pleasure was in turn a challenge to the Boggart, who knew that he became for that moment a small child showing off. *Look, I know how to fool you! Look at me!*

He reviewed his plans for the morning. He would start by throwing pans around in the kitchen, if nobody was there. Then he would squawl like a lovesick cat, drawing the attention even of Fergus' deaf ears, perhaps – and certainly of the MacDevon, who could never abide cats. When that brought the MacDevon out of his bed or his chair, the Boggart would take on the shape of a little black kitten, just for a moment, and run across the floor right past the MacDevon's feet – and then . . .

The Boggart hugged himself gleefully. He could see the MacDevon's face already: the astonishment, the outrage – and then the shamefaced incredulous laughter as he realized he had been tricked once more. *It's just you, is it then, my mannie? I'll be after you one of these days . . .*

He flittered away to the kitchen, which was indeed empty. In the sink, half filled with water, was a saucepan lined with congealed porridge. The Boggart reached for this pan and then decided against it; he was a fastidious creature, and disliked the idea of spraying gobbets of wet porridge all over the walls and floor. Instead he took half a dozen clean – though dusty – metal pots, and hurled them all round the kitchen with a sound like that of a car crashing into a wall.

He waited, grinning, for sounds of reaction from the MacDevon. But the castle was silent. The Boggart was disappointed, but not impatient. He could wait. He helped himself to an apple from the bowl on the kitchen table, and sat on the back of a chair, nibbling. The rays of sunshine which had been slanting through the kitchen's one small window disappeared, as a cloud bank swallowed the sun. The kitchen grew dark, and the Boggart felt lonely. Finishing his apple, he flittered to the MacDevon's bedroom, and like a small cloud of smoke he drifted in through the partly open door.

Nobody was there. The early sunshine must have wakened the MacDevon too. The Boggart made his way to the living room, smiling with anticipation, and began first to whimper and then to yowl like a cat in the corridor outside. Changing shape again, he trickled through the gap under the door and into the room, and looked up. Then he paused.

The MacDevon was sitting in his chair, smiling a little, with his eyes closed, and the dog Fergus lay across his feet, snoring gently. The fire in the hearth was cold ash. The Boggart looked at the two still figures and felt suddenly nervous. He made a loud abrupt cat sound.

Fergus stirred, and raised his head, but the MacDevon did not move. The old dog got shakily to his feet, and nudged with his muzzle at the limp hand lying on the MacDevon's knee, but still the MacDevon did not move. Then Fergus' animal instinct told him what had happened, and he put back his head and howled a wailing eerie howl, and hearing it, the Boggart knew that the MacDevon was dead.

He stayed there all day in the room, staring at the MacDevon, without stirring, without making a sound, as if by stillness he could prevent the passing of time. In his heart he felt a terrible ache, the ache he had sworn he would never feel again. The old dog Fergus howled and howled, a long ululation of mourning, as the sun rose and crossed the sky and began to sink to the west. Over on the mainland Tommy Cameron, walking home from the school bus, lifted his head and heard a faint murmur of the howling carried on the breeze. But Fergus was inside a room with ancient stone walls two feet thick, and the sound was not distinct. Tommy decided it was the passing of a flight of geese.

As the castle grew dark, Fergus's howls changed to whimpers, and at length he put his head down again on the MacDevon's feet, and slept. All the night long the Boggart stayed silent in the room, keeping vigil, fighting the pain of loss. When the darkness was eased by a growing light in the narrow windows of the room, and birds began faintly to chirp outside, the Boggart stirred himself and went to the kitchen to fetch food and a bowl of water for the dog.

But Fergus only raised his head, whimpered a little, and laid it down again on the MacDevon's feet. He would neither eat nor drink. He was a very old dog, held in life only by the thread of his devotion to his master, and without that he had no wish at all to live. So very soon he drifted into a deep sleep where his breathing grew gradually slower and more faint, and the Boggart knew that he had chosen not to wake up again.

Night fell, and Castle Keep was in darkness once more. The Boggart found candles and matches, and he lit a candle in every window of the great square grey home of the last MacDevon. In his misery he wanted to sleep as Fergus slept, but he was a boggart, and boggarts do not die. Out of an anguish of loneliness and loss he howled into the night as the dog had howled, keening a lament for his friend. And gradually the sound of his mourning changed, and became a chilling echo of the time he had felt another loving grief, centuries before. So all night long Tommy Cameron and all the other villagers tossed in their safe mainland beds, as they heard through their sleep, echoing over the water from the castle of the MacDevon, the plaintive wail of a single bagpipe, the creaking of a cart, the slow muffled shuffling of many feet, and the unending steady beat of a drum.

CHAPTER TWO

EMILY PUT her head around Jessup's door, ignoring, as usual, the large black-lettered banner reading DEATH TO ALL INVADERS. 'Get up, Idle,' she said.

Her brother pulled the sheet over his ears and made a snarling sound.

'It's ten o'clock!' said Emily. She bent down and let loose her secret weapon, the black kitten Polydore, known as Polly. The kitten gave a small mew of delight and rushed at Jessup's bed. It leaped lightly on to his pillow and began burrowing down under the sheet. Jessup shrieked.

Polly flew through the air and made a four-point landing on the wooden floor. She slid a little way, looking reproachfully at the bed.

Jessup surfaced. 'Get her out of here! She'll shed hairs in my computer!'

'You'll just have to train her not to,' Emily said unfeelingly. It was their first day home in Toronto after two barefoot seaside weeks in a cottage on Prince Edward Island, and nobody was pleased with life. Their parents had both disappeared to work, with a very bad grace, and Emily and Jessup were grumpily contemplating three dusty city weeks before school began. The most maladjusted of all the members of the family was Polly the kitten, who could not understand why she was surrounded by furniture instead of being out chasing grasshoppers and crabs beside the sea.

Emily surveyed her young brother's bedroom, which as always seemed to her unnaturally adult for the room of a ten-year-old. It was so full of sleek electronic equipment – computer, keyboard, printer, neat piles of games – that the bed looked out of place. She said, 'Get up, and I'll make you scrambled eggs.'

'Yay!' said Jessup, jumping out of bed.

'And take a shower.'

'No way. I'm not dirty.'

Emily had opened her mouth to argue when the telephone rang downstairs. She sprinted down to her parents' bedroom, with the kitten bounding after her.

A metallic voice at the other end of the line asked curtly for her father.

'He's not here,' Emily said. 'You can get him at –'

The voice interrupted her, sounding cross. 'Can I leave him a message?'

'Sure,' said Emily. She scrabbled for pencil and paper.

'He's at the theatre,' said Jessup, behind her, pulling on a T-shirt. 'Who is it?'

'Shush.' Emily was carefully taking dictation, her ear pressed to the telephone. She hung up. 'It was someone very . . .' Her voice trailed away, as she stared at what she had written.

Jessup peered at the paper. ' "You have inherited Castle Keep from Devon MacDevon," ' he read. ' "Please call reversed charge six-two-one-five-seven-eight-zero-three-three-five, Scotland. Signed Mac something." Mac what?'

'Maconochie. They spelled it out for me.'

'A castle?' Jessup said.

Emily let out a small mad giggle. 'It's like a card in Monopoly. "You have inherited a castle. Advance to Park Avenue. If you pass Go collect two hundred dollars." '

'A *castle*?'

'I'm calling Dad.'

But their father's line was busy. Quite forgetting the scrambled eggs, they shut a protesting Polly in the kitchen and ran through the leafy summer streets to the theatre.

Robert Volnik was the artistic director of the Chervil Playhouse, a small lively theatre which presented six plays a year in a converted Toronto broom factory. Having begun his career as an actor he still appeared in one or two of these productions – 'to use the muscles,' he said – but spent most of his days reading scripts, attending meetings and trying to raise money. Though he was a passionate amateur gardener he seldom had time to work in his tiny city garden, and reluctantly bribed Emily and Jessup to do the weeding instead. He was a stocky, cheerful man with thinning brown hair and a grey beard; his wife Maggie was lean and graceful and slightly taller than he, especially when wearing high heels. With a friend as partner, she ran an antiques shop called Old Stuff. Maggie and Robert had raised Emily and Jessup in a rather absent-minded way, treating them always as if they were small but grown-up colleagues on much the same level as the actors at Robert's theatre or the customers at Maggie's shop.

Robert sat now in his small office, its wall papered with posters and photographs, and blinked at Emily over his half-glasses. 'Castle Keep?' he said. 'I thought a keep was part of a castle.'

'It is,' said Jessup promptly. 'It's the tower, the strongest bit.'

Emily whacked impatiently at the message lying on Robert's desk. 'Dad! Call them up!'

Robert looked down again at the piece of paper. 'Mom!' he said. 'That's it. It must be my mother's side of the family. She was Scottish, she came over when she was three.'

'I thought she came from Edinburgh?' Jessup said.

'She did.' Robert sighed wistfully. 'I've always wanted to go there. Think of all the plays I might find at the Edinburgh Festival!'

Emily tugged distractedly at a strand of her long fair hair. Robert and Jessup were like squirrels; they would chew their way methodically through the shell of any problem, leaving a neat pile of little fragments, before arriving at the alluring kernel inside. It was the women in the Volnik family who were more direct. Maggie and Emily dealt with most matters as a seagull deals with a clam: choose a rock, fly up high, drop the clam on the rock, and thwack! It's open!

She picked up her father's telephone and dialled for the operator. 'Hello? Can you tell me how to call Scotland, please? And what does reversed charge mean?'

'Collect,' said the operator crisply. 'Give me the number, eh?'

Robert said, 'But Mom was an only child. Didn't even have any cousins that I ever heard of.'

'Maybe it's Edinburgh Castle!' Jessup said, his eyes gleaming.

In Emily's ear a very Scottish voice said, very faintly, as if it were on the moon, 'Mr Maconochie's office. Halloo?'

Emily handed the telephone wordlessly to her father.

A large, elderly golden retriever ambled into the office and butted at her legs. She reached out and patted him. 'Hi, Fred.'

Fred made the strange grunting, whining noise that was his usual greeting.

'Out!' said Robert, his brow furrowed as he tried to listen to Scotland.

They took the retriever out into the lobby. Fred

was the theatre dog. He belonged to Louise Spring, the general manager, a busy, bouncy lady with cropped white hair. Since Louise seemed to work sixteen hours a day at the Chervil Playhouse, Fred was always there too, wandering in and out of offices, dressing rooms and rehearsals. Once he had wandered onstage, during a school matinee of *Julius Caesar*, just as the conspirators were about to murder Caesar. He had barked loudly, tugging at Brutus' toga as he raised his dagger for the stabbing, and Caesar, dying, found himself uttering the line, 'Et tu, Brute?' into Fred's warm anxious brown eyes. The audience of children had cheered, delighted, but Fred was thereafter tied up in Mrs Spring's office during performances. As a consolation he was added to the list of technical staff in the theatre programmes. 'Security Guard,' it read, 'Fred Spring.'

Fred nuzzled Emily's hand, and then paused, sniffing at it with distaste.

'What's the matter?' she said to him, hurt.

'It's Polly,' Jessup said. 'He's never smelled cat on you before. Thinks you've gone over to the enemy.'

Fred gave Emily a look of disgust and ambled away to someone else's office. Jessup and Emily peered cautiously around their father's door.

Robert was sitting staring into space.

'Are you all right?' said Emily.

Their father turned his head towards them, but he still seemed to be somewhere else. 'It's a castle in the Western Highlands of Scotland. On a little island, part of a place called Appin.'

'Robert Louis Stevenson!' said Jessup in delight.

'What?'

'His book, *Kidnapped*. Mrs Stewart's reading it in class. Appin is where David Balfour and Alan Breck hide from the rrrrrredcoats in the heatherrrrrr.' He rolled the Rs theatrically, trying to make his father smile.

But Robert wasn't smiling. He looked harassed.

'Mr Maconochie is a lawyer,' he said. 'He was Devon MacDevon's lawyer. That's the old codger who's popped off in the castle. Mr M says that MacDevon was my grandmother's brother and that I'm his only heir. And he wants me to go over there.'

'We're rich!' said Emily in awe.

'How can I go to Scotland?' said her father plaintively. 'We've only just come back from the cabin. I've got meetings – and the grant proposals to write – and no, we're not rich at all, Mr Maconochie says the castle's falling down. Nobody in their right mind will want to buy it.'

'Buy it?' said Jessup, horrified. 'You've inherited our ancestral home! You surely don't want to sell it already!'

Their father looked even more worried. 'Well, that's the trouble,' he said unhappily. 'No, I don't.'

'Then you mustn't,' Maggie said firmly. 'We'll manage. Rent out the deer-hunting rights, or something.'

'There's no land,' Robert said. 'Just the castle.'

'Falling down,' added Emily.

They were all sitting in the late sunshine on the back steps of Maggie's shop, eating takeaway Chinese food with chopsticks out of leaky cardboard cartons. Maggie's partner, a chubby, grey-haired lady known to the children as Aunt Jen, sat with them, spooning up yoghurt. Aunt Jen was always on a diet, which never seemed to have any effect. She and Maggie were working late, taking inventory (or as Jen described it, 'counting the stuff'), so Robert, Emily and Jessup had brought them dinner and the news.

'This guy was your great-uncle?' Aunt Jen said, licking her spoon hungrily. 'He must have been ancient.'

'And lonely,' Robert said. 'He lived there all on

his own, Mr Maconochie said. No wife, no children, no anyone. One sister, but she ran away to Edinburgh when she was young and married someone from the wrong clan, so that was the last he heard of her. He never even mentioned her, except in his will. Mr Maconochie had to track her down – and he found she emigrated to Canada in 1923, with her husband and three-year-old daughter.'

'Grannie!' cried Emily, entranced. She could faintly remember her grandmother, as a fragrant, soft-cheeked presence who had died when she was five.

'The three-year-old, yes. My mom. Mary Campbell, who married Peter Volnik from Estonia.'

'Almost as romantic as her Canadian son marrying an English girl from Manchester,' said Maggie in her lingering English accent, smiling at her husband. Robert leaned sideways behind Jessup, and kissed her on the ear.

'You're dripping shrimp foo yong down my neck,' Jessup said coldly.

'And in the third generation, romance dies,' Robert said, sitting back. 'Pass the fried rice, Jessup.'

Aunt Jen dug her spoon into the fried rice as it went by. She said, 'Whether or not you keep this ancestral pile, you know, you do have to go over there.'

Robert groaned. 'I can't afford to!'

'Fares are getting lower, this time of year.'

'It's the time I can't afford. Money's no problem, for once – Mr Mac said the estate could pay.'

'That means you, if it's your estate.'

'Oh well,' Robert said.

Aunt Jen stole another spoonful of rice. 'Maggie should go with you. The castle might be full of antiques. I'd mind the store.'

'What about us?' said Jessup plaintively.

Inside the shop, a loud buzzer sounded, indicating that someone had come through the front door. Emily and Jessup shot to their feet, looking hopeful.

'Oh Lord,' said Aunt Jen. 'Customer. I forgot to close up.'

Maggie looked at her children, and grinned. 'The double act, eh? OK – but keep it short.'

They scurried indoors. Emily glanced at her hair in the mirror, and peered down to make sure Jessup's T-shirt was tucked into his jeans. Then she opened the pass door and the two of them went side by side into the shop. Being crammed with furniture, it looked like a very crowded living room, with a few eccentric patches like the row of four grandfather clocks against one wall, or the cluster of six chandeliers in a corner of the ceiling.

A tall thin man with a lot of dark hair was bent over a table, reading its price tag. Emily took Jessup's hand. It was a signal; at once they began speaking in unison.

'Good evening.'

The tall man straightened abruptly. 'Good evening,' he said. He wore a charcoal-grey business suit, very well cut, and a tie.

'Welcome to Old Stuff,' said Emily and Jessup together.

'A Greek chorus,' said the tall man coolly. 'How very suitable for an antiques shop.'

Emily sensed that Jessup was about to depart from the script, so she squeezed his hand firmly and they went on, perfectly synchronized. 'Please let us know if we can answer any questions.'

The man's dark brows drew together, and Emily took a sudden dislike to him. *No sense of humour*, she thought.

'Not a question – a request,' he said shortly. 'Go get your mother.'

Before Emily could move, Jessup had swung away from her and opened the door to the back of the house. 'Mom!' he called in his clear light voice. 'There's a bad-tempered man here to see you.'

Maggie came warily into the shop and found the dark-haired man and her children eyeing each other in chilly silence. He said when he saw her, 'This seems an excellent way to lose a good customer.'

Maggie smiled at him. 'I do hope you're a good customer. And that we shan't lose you.'

The man pulled a folded newspaper from his jacket-pocket. 'You advertised a roll-top desk?'

Emily's spirits fell. She had fallen in love with the roll-top desk, which had been in the shop for four weeks now. She had been hoping nobody would buy it, so that her mother might be persuaded to give it to her as a Christmas present.

'Over here,' said her treacherous mother, and led the tall man to Emily's desk. He rolled the deliciously smooth-moving top up and down, poked at the engaging array of little compartments inside, got down on his hands and knees (after first spreading his newspaper fastidiously on the floor) and peered up at the bottom of the desk.

'Fifteen hundred dollars,' Maggie said. 'It's Victorian – in excellent condition.'

Emily felt more hopeful. Surely no one would pay that much.

'I'll give you a thousand,' said the tall man.

'Twelve hundred,' Maggie said.

'Done!' he said quickly. He stood up. 'Will you take a cheque?'

Emily thought: *Say no. Don't trust him. Say no.*

'Of course,' said her mother happily.

Disgusted, Emily slipped away through the pass door and found Jessup at her side.

'What a creep!' he said.

Emily made a loud, graphic vomiting sound.

Their father and Aunt Jen were sitting together on the back steps finishing the fried rice. Robert looked up, pained. 'Please!' he said.

'Well, he's an awful man. And Mom's just sold him that pretty desk.'

'Oh good!' said Aunt Jen. 'How much?'

'Twelve hundred dollars.'

'Terrific!'

Emily said with dignity, 'I think it's disgusting to have to be sweet and gushy to creepy people just so you can sell them something.'

'Oh darling,' said her father sadly, 'it's the way of the world. Louise and I will be gushy to almost anyone if they'll give us money to keep the Playhouse alive.'

'Well, I'm not going to spend *my* life doing that.'

'She wants to be an environmental lawyer, at present,' Robert said to Aunt Jen. 'I'm going to come listen when she has to persuade some billionaire to finance her saving the whales.'

Maggie appeared on the steps, waving a cheque. 'He wasn't so bad,' she said to her children. 'He's a psychiatrist, Dr William Stigmore. Has an office on Avenue Road. He wants us to find him a bookcase to match the desk.'

'He's a creep,' said Jessup.

'I think you're getting too old for that double-child act,' his mother said ominously. 'It's not cute any more.' Then she grinned at them. 'Anyway look at this. Dr Stigmore left his newspaper on the floor, and look at the ad I found staring up at me!'

She spread the paper on the steps, folded to show a half-page advertisement for an airline. It was full of large black type and exclamation marks. FLY YOUR KIDS TO BRITAIN! it said. And then in smaller print: ONE PARENT, ONE CHILD FOR ONE ADULT FARE!

'Autumn Special. I checked it online. Bargain flights to London, if you go before November,' Maggie said. 'How about it, Robert? Take ten days off before the season swallows you up? Solve the castle problem? Show the children their ethnic background?'

Emily and Jessup stared at her, wide-eyed. Emily said, 'You mean you'd take us?'

'Well, well,' said Robert. 'See how useful a creep can be?'

CHAPTER THREE

I T WAS only as the big plane rose into the air that Jessup really believed what was happening to him. He felt his body tilted upward, pressed back against the seat by acceleration; he felt a pain in his ears as air hissed into the cabin to balance the thinner outside atmosphere into which they were climbing.

'Swallow,' said his father in his ear, and Jessup swallowed and the pain went away. Outside the window he saw the shoreline of Lake Ontario tilting crazily as the plane banked away from Toronto. He peeked back through the gap between his seat and the window, and caught a glimpse of Emily's face pressed intent against the glass. 'Psst!' he said softly, joyously. 'We're going to Scotland!'

'Psst yourself,' said Emily calmly. 'Of course we are.'

But later, hours later, forty thousand feet over the Atlantic Ocean, she changed places with Robert so that children and grown-ups could each sit with their own kind, and she gazed past Jessup out of the window and whispered, 'Look! They're like mountains!' And Jessup too looked at the limitless world of mounded cloud tops below them, glimmering in the last light from the sunset they had left behind, and he knew she was as deeply excited as he was himself. He poked her in the ribs with his elbow, and they grinned at each other.

The half-buried feeling of wonder lasted for a long time, through the airline dinners of which they ate every scrap of their own, and their parents' desserts as well; through a film which they had seen before but laughed at all over again; through sleep broken by an airline hostess offering them orange juice and a bagel far sooner than they wanted them. But they ate and drank just the same, and soon found themselves looking down at a dim-lit layer of cloud dappling the misty green floor that was morning Britain.

Mist was their main impression for quite a

while after that. They had dropped into a grey, damp world. A fine rain was falling on Heathrow Airport, where they waited sleepily in line with hundreds of other Canadians and Americans to show their passports at the immigration desk. At length they were beckoned forward as a family group, by an immigration officer with bright red hair and freckles. Jessup felt restive. *We're not just tourists*, he thought, *we're different!* He stood on tiptoe, straining to see over the desk, as the officer surveyed them all.

'What's the purpose of your visit – business or pleasure?' said the officer, to Robert.

'Pleasure, I hope,' said Robert.

'We're going to take over our castle in Scotland,' Jessup said proudly. Emily kicked him, and he kicked back at her without looking, and missed.

The immigration officer looked down at him gravely. 'Are you now? Well, just remember that if you take it home you'll need an export licence.' He stamped their passports and waved them through.

'He didn't believe me,' said Jessup bitterly, as they went down the stairs to wait for their luggage.

'Didn't you hear his accent?' said Emily. 'You dummy – he was *Scottish*!'

*

It was a day and a night before they heard other Scottish voices. Following a plan which Maggie had devised with the help of a Toronto travel agent, they piled their suitcases into a rented car at the airport and drove to a small hotel in London. There, after breakneck visits to the Zoo, Queen Mary's Rose Garden and the Royal National Theatre, they spent the night. Next morning they watched the Changing of the Guard, with the shade of Christopher Robin hovering over them, and tried to concentrate on sightseeing, in the old grey city which seemed to have almost as many trees and tall new buildings as Toronto. But all four of them knew that London was only an interlude; that their adventure would not really begin until they reached Scotland. Nobody was sorry when in their second afternoon they filled the car with luggage once more and drove to Euston Station, where their car was swallowed up inside a railway carriage with one end gaping open, like a huge hungry mouth.

Emily and Jessup spent their second British night in a private space which they found entrancing: a sleeping compartment, opening off the corridor which ran along one side of the train. It was a tiny rocking room with a door, a window, a table which folded up to reveal a very small washbasin with hot and cold water, and two bunk beds neatly made up with sheets, blankets and pillows. After a picnic supper in their parents' identical compartment next door, they tossed to see who got the upper bunk, and Jessup won. Emily didn't mind: it was easier to see out of the window from the lower bunk. She fell asleep very soon, rocked by the rhythm of the moving train and lulled by the travelling song of its wheels. Once, in the middle of the night, she woke up and found the train standing still. Peeking under the blind, she saw the empty, brightly lit platform of a station, with no sign to show her where she was. Emily felt wonderfully detached; the train had taken over her life, whisking her from strange place to strange place in this foreign country. She fell asleep again, and dreamed that she was a bird, flying over cities and rivers and mountains. In her dream she could see the train moving along the ground far below her, like a tiny slow-moving snake, and the sound of the wind rushing by her as she flew was like the song of the travelling wheels. She woke, and found that she was smiling.

And outside the window, the world had changed entirely. The train was carrying them now through dark looming hills, ancient smooth slopes with the glint of water beyond, and the sky behind them brightening. As she watched from her swaying bed, the sun rose, and magically colour came into the land, showing her purple-brown hillsides and green fields against a blue-white sky. Emily felt suddenly very excited, as if amazing things were about to happen, and she wanted to wake Jessup and tell him. But instead she was wrapped again by drowsiness, and in the moment that her eyes closed, she heard music. It was the lilt of a single Scottish bagpipe, far away, plaintive and beautiful, but before Emily could fix it in her memory she had dropped into sleep.

The train stood hissing in Fort William Station, in the Western Highlands of Scotland, and they could see nothing for the rain. Water streamed down the windows, and blew all over them as they opened the door, and they scurried along the cold windy platform towards shelter, clutching their overnight bags.

'Welcome to Scotland!' said Maggie, gasping as they reached the station buildings. 'Oh – excuse me –!' She had almost knocked down a small man in railway uniform; he put a polite hand under her arm to steady her.

'It is a wet morning,' said the small man rather

unnecessarily, in the soft musical lilt of the Highlands. 'Do you have a motorcar on this train?'

'Yes!' said Jessup eagerly. 'We're driving to Port Appin!' He shook his wet head, like a puppy.

'Over the other side,' the man said amiably, pointing. 'But they will be a little while getting them off. You'd maybe like some breakfast in the refreshment room.'

'Great!' said Emily, and she dragged her brother away before he could begin to tell the man about their castle. She was learning to recognize the signs: the possessive light in Jessup's eye, the breath taken before launching into proud explanation. She felt that if he wasn't careful, a band of jealous Scots, hearing about their bequest, would rise up and throw the whole invading Volnik family out of the country.

'You've got to stop bragging to people about the castle!' she said, as they reached the warm, food-smelling refuge of a cafeteria.

'I never said a word!' Jessup said, injured.

'You were just going to.'

'How do you know?'

'Enough!' said Robert imperiously. He bought them bacon sandwiches and Coke, and coffee for Maggie, and with a noble self-sacrificing sigh he turned up the collar of his windcheater and went out into the driving rain to rescue their car.

Emily looked out through the wet window at Fort William. It seemed a grey town, bleak and deserted. She said, 'Mom, d'you think we should take some sandwiches with us?'

'Oh no, darling,' said her mother confidently. 'After all, we're going to our house!'

'Our *castle*,' Jessup said.

It was one of those journeys that are taken over by the weather. They were vaguely aware that they were driving beside water, and among mountains, and that the countryside would have been beautiful if only they had been able to see it. But all they could properly see was the rain, running in sheets down the windows of the car, so that the windscreen wipers had to flicker furiously to and fro like runners who couldn't quite keep up. Even when the downpour slackened to a drizzle, the clouds hung low and ragged, masking the hills with mist. Robert was hunched over the steering wheel, concentrating on his left-hand-side driving, and beside him Maggie was intent on the map.

'Through North Ballachulish, and over Loch

Leven to Portnacroish – and then you turn left at Appin –'

The names were magical, Emily thought: a different language, a different world. But what a pity it had to be such a wet world. They drove for a long time. Her spirits were beginning to droop in the grey mistiness, and beside her Jessup was very silent.

They were driving along a narrower road now, between hedges and green banks, no longer meeting many other cars. The mist was patchier, more ragged. Sometimes it vanished altogether, and they had a clear sight of water glimmering nearby, with dark mountains beyond.

'That's Loch Linnhe,' Maggie said, checking with her map. 'And somewhere in it there's a long skinny island called Lismore.'

They rounded a bend, and came into low-lying land like the flats around the estuary of a river. And suddenly the mist was completely gone, as if it had rolled back towards the mountains across the water, and a few hundred yards away, rising from the glinting grey surface of the loch, they saw a tall square shape set on a lonely rock. It was like a squat grey stone tower, and yet it was not a tower, but had a round tower of its own built at one corner. It had windows like a house, but the windows were very few and very small. It was like nothing they had ever seen before, and though the rock on which it stood was undoubtedly an island, being completely surrounded by water, it was a very small island indeed.

'Is that Lismore Island?' Emily said doubtfully.

Maggie's voice was quivering a little with excitement. She said, 'I think that must be Castle Keep.'

'Indeed yes, Mr Maconochie left the key for you,' said Mrs Cameron. 'Though Tommy tells me the lock does not work very well, because it was never used when Mr MacDevon was alive. Or ever before that, I dare say.'

Emily and Jessup looked at Tommy, who had himself been looking at them and now glanced hastily away. They were all three in that warily inquisitive stage after first meeting a stranger, when if people were dogs they would be walking around one another, sniffing. At the moment Emily and Jessup were mentally sniffing at the news that Tommy was an authority on the lock of Castle Keep. *Their* castle. They weren't sure whether to be outraged or impressed.

Mr Maconochie had instructed Robert to ask for the key at Mrs Cameron's shop, but he would have ended up there anyway, for there were only two shops in the whole of Port Appin and Mrs Cameron's was the only one that sold groceries. All the Volniks had instantly fallen in love with it; there was everything you could want in this shop, from bread to books, from fruit to flour, from nails to knitting needles. One corner of its counter even served as the local post office. It was small and very crowded, and through the window facing the loch you could look out past a neat array of fifteen different kinds of Scotch whisky bottles and see Castle Keep.

'Tommy will take you over in the boat,' Mrs Cameron said. She was a short, precise woman, wearing an apron that was clearly newly ironed. Like her shop, she looked ferociously clean.

'That's very kind,' Robert said.

'I guess I should do my shopping first,' Maggie said. 'We'll be here for five days. I have a list somewhere –' She began fumbling through her handbag.

'You are intending to stay in the castle?' Mrs Cameron said. She seemed startled.

'You bet!' said Jessup.

Maggie paused. 'Is there any reason why we shouldn't?'

'Oh no, no!' said Mrs Cameron, almost too quickly. 'It's just . . . there's no electricity. And, there may not be beds enough. Mr MacDevon lived there alone all his life.'

'We brought sleeping bags,' Jessup said. 'We're used to camping out.' He looked at Mrs Cameron defensively, and so did Emily; no power in Scotland was going to stop them from sleeping in Castle Keep.

Mrs Cameron said, as if it were an explanation, 'He was a very old gentleman. Very old indeed.'

Tommy said abruptly, in a rather gruff voice, 'He kept the place clean as a pin.'

'Oh yes,' said his mother. She patted him gently on the shoulder.

'It was only the dog that smelled,' Tommy said.

'Oh!' said Emily, pleased. 'Is there a dog?'

'He died,' Mrs Cameron said.

'Here's my list!' said Maggie. She pulled a crumpled piece of paper triumphantly from her bag.

'I'll go and get the boat,' said Tommy, and his mother nodded quickly. It was almost as if she wanted to get rid of him, Emily thought.

Jessup said, 'Can we come too?'

There was a moment's pause, while he and Emily stared hopefully at the other boy. They saw curly black hair and a sunburned nose, and very blue eyes.

'All right,' Tommy said.

He led them out of the shop, past the rack of bicycles and along a road of small quiet houses, with roses and hollyhocks bright in their gardens even in late August.

'I'm Emily,' Emily said. 'He's Jessup.'

'Yes,' said Tommy. He walked in silence for a few moments. 'When did you come from America?' he said.

Emily said, 'Actually we came from Canada.'

'Two days ago,' said Jessup. 'The plane was really cool, it had these little screens at every seat for the movie, like your own TV.'

'Like a computer screen,' Tommy said.

Emily said, and wished to die as she heard herself saying it, 'You have a computer?'

The blue eyes flicked to her for a cold instant. 'My father does. This is Scotland you're in, not deepest Africa.'

'I'm sorry. Jess is such a computer geek, but I'm not, so I don't expect anyone else to be either . . .' She thought: *Shut up, you're making it worse.*

Jessup said, 'What was Mr MacDevon like?'

'Old,' Tommy said. 'And quiet. As if he belonged to some other time. He was a very decent man.'

'Was he really a hundred years old?'

'So they said.'

Emily said, 'He was our great-great-uncle, I guess.'

Tommy Cameron said calmly, 'You are not like him at all.'

Emily was on the edge of feeling insulted when the houses gave way to a pebbly beach, and she found herself looking out at the whole glimmering expanse of the loch and the hills beyond. Mounded grey clouds filled the sky, and from behind one of them a watery ray of sunshine reached out to a chunky high-bowed boat, moving towards them with a rippling wake spreading behind it in a great V.

'Oh!' Emily said, enchanted.

Tommy said, more gently, 'That is the ferry from Lismore.'

Jessup stuck doggedly to his subject, as usual. 'What did Mr MacDevon die of?'

'Old age, of course,' Tommy said, curt again. He strode out along a stone jetty, where a few people were waiting for the ferry, and reached down to untie the painter of a small dinghy with an outboard motor at its stern. 'Here,' he said, and stood holding the line as Emily and Jessup scrambled down into the boat. 'Jessup in front. You'll have to jump out when we hit the beach.'

It was a noisy little engine, and they did not talk while the boat chugged around the rocky shore to the tiny beach which was the nearest point to the Camerons' shop. Emily could not take her eyes off the silent grey shape of Castle Keep, out over the still water. She turned, startled, as Tommy suddenly stopped the engine, tilted it forward, and in the same moment called to Jessup and came leaping lightly past her to jump out and guide the boat as it nosed into the beach. She scrambled after him, anxious to be helpful. Tommy was clearly about her own age, but in the boat he seemed like an adult, automatically taking charge. And there was something oddly serious about him, all the time.

They tugged the boat on to the beach. Up on the road they could see Robert coming towards them from the shop, carrying a box of groceries.

Tommy paused, looking out at Castle Keep. He said abruptly, 'He died in his sleep. Just wore out, because he was so old. It was a Monday, and I took the boat over with his Sunday paper, like I always did. We had seen him two days before – he rowed over to do his shopping. But there was not a sound in the castle, so I went calling for him, and I found him sitting in his chair, with his dog lying across his feet. And they were both dead.'

'Wow!' said Jessup, big-eyed.

Emily said, 'Weren't you scared?'

Tommy looked at her, expressionless. He thought of the sounds he had heard that previous night from the castle, the heartrending sounds of the Boggart's grief. He might have tried to explain how it was possible not to be afraid because you were too busy being sorry for someone. But there was no way he was going to tell these two foreigners about the Boggart.

He said, 'I just felt there was a great sadness about the place.'

Robert dropped the box on the beach at their feet. He said, 'There are four more of these – Maggie seems to think we're staying for a month. Your mother feels you'll need two trips, Tommy – maybe you should take the kids and me over first, and then come back for Mrs Volnik and the rest of the stuff.'

'OK,' Tommy said. 'Jump in.'

He put Robert and the box in the middle of the boat, Jessup in the bow and Emily beside him in the stern, and the little dinghy rode low but steady in the water as he motored carefully off.

Jessup stared at Castle Keep as it loomed up before them; he felt solitary and daring, like the hero of *Kidnapped* on his first visit to the sinister house of Shaws. But Castle Keep looked lonely and bereft, rather than sinister. As soon as the boat nosed up to its rocky shore, he seized the line and jumped out, finding an iron ring set into the rock that faced him. Jessup tied the line to it quickly as Robert and Emily came past him, and then looked up at Tommy.

He thought rather smugly that he might see surprised approval on Tommy's face for the bowline knot that he had tied, but instead Tommy was looking at him with a queer mixture of anticipation and envy. He said, 'That's the first foot with MacDevon blood in it that's trod this rock since the old man died.'

In the stone wall of the MacDevon's study, high above the bookshelves with their rows of dusty leatherbound books, the Boggart stirred. From the depths of his ancient wild mind a threadlike voice had called to him, though he had not heard it, nor felt any cause for his waking. When he opened his eyes, his first instinct was to close them again, fast, and go back to sleep before he could feel the pain of loss that lay waiting for him like a dark dank cloud. As a thing of the Wild Magic, this was his right; the compensation for perpetual life was the ability to retreat from it, to take refuge in a deep, bodiless sleep for days or weeks or years. Even for centuries. His cousin the Boggart of Loch Ness, who liked to take on so large and awful a shape that humans called him the Monster, was well known for sleeping nearly all the time. He would swim up to the surface of his loch only once or twice a year, for the sake of surprising the fish and of frustrating any passing tourist caught without his camera.

The Boggart curled back towards sleep again, like a snail pulling its horns and body into its shell. He had no desire yet to face a world without the MacDevon in it. But something was tugging him into wakefulness, some unheard call, demanding obedience.

He lay there resentfully awake, listening.

Maggie Volnik stood in the kitchen of Castle Keep, gazing around her with undisguised dismay.

Plaster was flaking from the walls, lying in little piles of dirty white fragments on the bare stone floor and the bare wooden countertops, and there were dead flies and mouse droppings in the two enormous stone sinks. A few china mugs and plates, jugs and bowls were set on the wooden shelves that lined one wall, and several saucepans hung from a big wrought-iron circle suspended from the ceiling. Other pots and pans lay on the floor beneath a vast central table, its wooden surface hollowed by centuries of scrubbing. They had lain there ever since the day the Boggart had thrown them happily around the kitchen, just before he found the MacDevon dead.

This was the first time Tommy had been in the kitchen since then. He had been keeping away, to leave the Boggart undisturbed with his grief. He said, looking nervously around at the chaos, 'I'd have come and cleaned the place up, if we'd known you would be staying here.'

'I expect there's a broom,' Maggie said bleakly.

'Oh yes. Mr MacDevon was a very tidy man. And there is running water here in the kitchen, and gas for the stove and the lights. It comes from a big tank outside, the boat brings a new one every three months.'

'Gas lamps!' said Robert in wonder, gazing at the walls.

Tommy showed him how to light one, holding a lighted match and cautiously turning the tap until there was a *pop!* and the mantle inside the lamp began to glow. Emily and Jessup came in, carrying a box of groceries between them.

'Where's the fridge?' said Emily briskly.

'There's just the pantry,' Tommy said. He opened a door to reveal a capacious closet with a stone shelf set in it. Emily put the milk, eggs and butter on the shelf, looking doubtful. She said, 'I guess Mr MacDevon didn't buy ice cream.'

'Once in a while he did,' Tommy said. 'He would take it home wrapped in newspaper and eat it that night. He was very fond of vanilla ice cream, and so was the Bog–' He stopped himself just in time.

'The bog?' said Jessup.

'The dog,' Tommy said hastily. 'Fergus, the dog.'

Robert had been prowling the kitchen. 'There's no electricity in the castle, right? So no phone.'

'That is right. There are paraffin lamps for the bedrooms. Up there.' Tommy pointed to several dusty lanterns on the shelf.

'Paraffin?' said Jessup.

'Kerosene to you,' Maggie said.

'Did you use all those weird names when you were little?' Jessup wrinkled his nose. '*Roundabout* for *rotary*, and *lorry* for *truck* –'

'A rose by any other name would smell as sweet,' said Robert. 'So shut up. I need to learn how to light these lamps.'

'*I* need to explore the castle!' Jessup made for the door, and Emily darted after him. Tommy called to their vanishing backs, 'Keep away from the doors that are barred – they lead to the part that's falling down!'

They clattered from room to room, flinging open huge wooden doors, climbing up and down stone stairways, calling in excitement to each other as they discovered the living room with the MacDevon's tall wing chair, the bedrooms with their four-poster beds. 'Come see this!'

And then they flung open the door of the library.

'Wow!' cried Jessup. 'Look at all these books! And there's a globe – and an *astrolabe* –'

'A what?'

'It's an old instrument for measuring stars – look –'

Up in his space above the shelves, the Boggart winced at the loud young voices, and peered resentfully out past Volume One of *The Lays of Ancient Rome*. Who were these noisy disrespectful creatures with the strange accent? He knew the Boy from across the water; the Boy knew him too, and was properly irritated or amused by boggart tricks. But these two had no sense of propriety or place, clearly. He hoped they would go away, at once.

'Emily! Jessup!' Maggie's voice came from upstairs. She had been touring too, while Tommy and Robert fetched in a new boatload of sleeping bags and luggage. 'Hey, kids! Come choose bedrooms!'

They whooped, and disappeared. The Boggart pressed himself back into his space, wishing sleep were not so strangely unwilling to rescue him.

The door opened again, a little, and Tommy slipped in. He said to the air, tentatively, 'Boggart?'

There was no sound or movement in the room.

'They're harmless, they are really,' Tommy said. 'And they won't be here long.'

The Boggart sulked in silence. He thought: *Yes, I'll take good care they'll not be here long.*

CHAPTER FOUR

FOR THE Boggart, however, the Volniks' first night in Castle Keep was sadly frustrating. By the time he roused himself from his sulks in the library wall and flittered downstairs, Robert, Emily and Jessup had carried sleeping bags and suitcases up to the bedrooms and Maggie had cooked and served supper. The kitchen was full of a delicious smell of sausages and bacon, two of the Boggart's favourite foods, but he came into the room just in time to see the last forkful disappear into Jessup's mouth.

'That was great!' said Jessup indistinctly. He stuffed a piece of bread into his mouth to join the sausage. There was plenty of bread left on the table, but it was sliced bakery bread from the Camerons' shop, wrapped in plastic, and the Boggart looked at it with disdain. Compared to the wonderful coarse wholemeal bread the MacDevon had baked once a week, this was poor stuff.

The Boggart made his invisible way around the four plates, investigating. The smell made his mouth water, but there was nothing left that he thought worth eating. Boggarts need neither food nor drink to survive, but they relish certain things that catch their fancy. For centuries the Boggart had preferred the traditional favourites of his kind: oatcakes spread with butter or honey, and fresh cream to drink. A lifetime spent with the MacDevon, however, had broadened his taste to a range of things from fish fingers to ketchup. Once in a while he even enjoyed a dram of good Scotch whisky, which would put him to sleep for almost a week.

Frustrated and hungry, he was now suddenly furious with the Volniks, and overturned the milk jug on the table just as Jessup was reaching past it for more bread.

'Oh, Jessup!' said Maggie mildly. She righted the jug, which had been almost empty, and mopped up a few drops of milk with her paper napkin.

'It wasn't me,' said Jessup. He looked uncertainly at the jug. 'Was it?'

'Yes!' shouted the Boggart crossly, silently at Maggie, but in vain. She patted Jessup on the arm.

'Never mind,' she said benevolently. 'We're all tired. No harm done.'

The rest of the night went the same way. The Boggart could neither irritate nor aggravate anyone, nor find any way to make trouble. When he stole Maggie's hairbrush, she merely sighed and decided she must have left it in the car. When he tripped Emily up on her way to the huge four-poster bed she was to share with Jessup, she blamed a frayed rug instead of yelling angrily at her brother. And when the Boggart moaned heartrendingly on the landing in the dead of night, and made beautiful vivid sounds of clanking chains, nobody even noticed. They were all so exhausted from the journey that they remained fast asleep.

By sunrise the Boggart was exhausted too. He went sullenly back to the library wall and curled up in his hole, muttering curses which instantly vaporized an unfortunate passing mouse, but had no effect on his unwelcome foreign invaders at all.

While the Boggart slept for the next two days, Emily and Jessup fell in love with Port Appin.

They grew quickly bored inside the castle, since its rooms were in general small, dark, damp and very cold, and its more interesting tumbledown half was shut off from exploring by heavy beams of wood barring certain doors. So they roamed the beaches, rocks and caves of the mainland, sometimes in the rain, after being dropped by Robert in the boat he had rented from a local fisherman. Now and then Tommy joined them. He came puttering over to the castle regularly with telephone messages from the Edinburgh lawyer for Robert and Maggie, who were in long-distance consultation with Mr Maconochie, the Edinburgh lawyer.

On their fourth day in Castle Keep the sun came out, and the loch was transformed into a breathtaking picture-book place of blue water and sky, soft purple hills, and gleaming wet rocks and sand. Tommy took Emily and Jessup to a point of land facing the island of Lismore, with the bigger island of Mull misty behind it. Seaweed-draped boulders stretched down to the water, and to a scattering of great part-submerged rocks.

'Just stay still,' Tommy said, 'and watch.'

The sun warmed their faces, and the air was full of the soft lapping of the waves, and the distant calling of birds. There was a clean smell of the sea, and the tall rock where they sat was pillowed with green mounds of sea thrift, and pink nodding blossoms.

Suddenly Tommy grasped Emily's arm. He said softly, 'Look!'

From the water beyond them a head rose, a dog-shaped head, glistening and wet. Water dripped from its whiskers. Another rose beside it, and a dark bulky body with sloping shoulders hoisted itself up on to the rock in the sunshine. Great dark eyes were looking straight at Emily. She gazed back, spellbound.

Jessup cried joyously, 'Seals!'

Almost before the word was out of his mouth the seals had slipped back into the water and disappeared.

'They have special ways of closing their nostrils,' said Jessup, excited. 'They can stay under water for twenty minutes, without coming up for air!'

Emily thought with rueful affection: *You care more about the facts and figures than about watching the seals.* 'They have eyes like people,' she said dreamily. She smiled at Tommy.

The seals did not come out of the sea again. The children walked back along the rocks, the castle rising ahead of them. Tommy said in an odd, husky voice, 'They came up to see you. I have never known them come so fast, for anyone but Mr MacDevon. He used to say they were his kin.'

Emily paused. She said cautiously, 'My great-great-uncle said he was related to seals?'

'Do you not believe it?' Tommy said.

Emily thought of the big dark eyes, looking at her. She said, 'I don't know.'

Jessup was not listening. His mind was still darting about in its usual unpredictable fashion. He said suddenly to Tommy, 'Do you live in the shop?'

'On top of it,' Tommy said.

'D'you know Morse code?'

'Not very well,' Tommy said guardedly. 'Why?'

'The shop faces my bedroom window, in the castle. We could talk to each other, with flashlights.'

Tommy looked blank. 'What's a flashlight?'

'You don't have *flashlights*?' Jessup said. 'Jeeze! A cylinder, like, with batteries inside it, and a light bulb behind glass at one end –'

Tommy's blue eyes glinted dangerously. 'We have a thing in Scotland that's a cylinder too. Very thin, made of wood, with graphite in the centre. We call it a pencil.'

Jessup hooted. 'You think *we* don't have *pencils*?'

'*You think we don't have flashlights?*' Tommy snapped. 'That's just American dialect. In the English language they're called torches.'

Emily said mildly, 'Actually we're Canadians.'

The words dropped like a damp blanket over the heat the boys were beginning to generate, and they gaped at her. Then Tommy grinned. 'Hey, Canadian Jessup,' he said. 'If you're really a computer geek, how about helping to set up my dad's new one?'

Jessup's face lit up. He said happily, 'You bet!'

Mrs Cameron was counting out stamps at the post office counter when they went into the shop. Tommy said, 'D'you need me, Mum? Jessup's going to teach the computer how to speak American.'

Emily sighed. 'Canadian,' she said.

'That's nice,' said Mrs Cameron vaguely. 'Oh, Emily, dear – will you tell your parents Mr Maconochie will be here at ten tomorrow morning, to discuss the sale?'

Emily stared at her. 'What sale?'

'Darling,' said Maggie patiently, 'how on earth could we possibly keep the castle?'

'You wanted to,' Emily said accusingly to her father.

Robert looked unhappy, and tugged his beard. 'I'd need to be a millionaire, Em.'

'Toronto is a long way away,' Mr Maconochie said, looking down sympathetically at Emily. 'It is hard to take care of a place halfway across the world.' He had a deep voice, but soft and quiet, surprising in so tall a man. His face was long and lined, with thinning silver hair above it, and his dark business suit looked impractical next to everyone else's heavy sweaters and jeans. They had a coal fire glowing in the big fireplace of the main room, but the castle was still cold.

Mr Maconochie had arrived that morning, after driving from his law office in Edinburgh. He must have left very early, for he had been telling them how beautiful the hills had looked with the sun rising over them. He had sounded as excited and surprised as a small boy let unexpectedly out of school. Emily decided that she liked him; he was the kind of person who would understand how she had felt when she looked into the eyes of the seals.

Like the Volniks, Mr Maconochie had never seen Castle Keep before. It was his senior partner who had been Mr MacDevon's lawyer and written his will, and the partner had been dead for ten years. Maggie, who enjoyed talking to people about themselves, discovered over a welcoming cup of tea that Mr Maconochie was a peaceable bachelor in his sixties, living with a great many books and pictures and a housekeeper in his house in Edinburgh, where he ran the remaining law practice and dreamed vainly of fly fishing and long walks over the hills. He seemed as reluctant to have them sell the castle as they were themselves.

'Perhaps the National Trust for Scotland . . .' Mr Maconochie's voice trailed away, and he shook his head. 'No, alas. They couldn't afford to take the place without an endowment to keep it up.'

'Endowment?' Emily said.

'Money,' Robert said gloomily. 'The thing we're all short of.'

Mr Maconochie said with regret, 'I'm afraid you are right. There seems no alternative to putting it on the market.'

Maggie put some more coal on the fire. Tommy had shown them a cellar full of coal in an obscure corner of the castle; his father had seen a barge unload the coal years before, and said that two men had been occupied for a week shovelling it into the cellar. There was still enough left for half a lifetime.

'There are some beautiful bits of furniture,' Maggie said. 'Would it be all right for me to ship them home and sell them in Toronto?'

Mr Maconochie said formally, 'It's your furniture, Mrs Volnik, yours and your husband's. You may do anything with it that you wish.'

Maggie sat down cross-legged by the fire, and pushed her long hair out of her eyes. She smiled at him. 'But you think it should really stay in Scotland?'

The lawyer laughed – though rather sadly, Emily thought. He said, 'Scotland has been sending men and women to Canada for more than two hundred years – it's no crime to send a little furniture after them.'

There was a knock at the door, and Tommy came in. The door creaked and groaned as he pushed it open. 'I was looking for Jessup,' he said.

Emily jumped up. 'He's in the library. Can we show Mr Maconochie the books, Mom?'

So it was a troop of all of them that brought voices and footsteps into the dim-lit library, where Jessup was sitting beside a paraffin lamp reading a big book about Scottish railways, and filling the air incongruously with a blast of rock music from his Walkman.

The Boggart was pressed far back into his high

refuge above the shelves, curled in a ball like an animal trying to hibernate. The beat of the music was like a physical pain that he could not escape, and he had been growing more and more resentful and angry. But there was no way out: Jessup had shut the door behind him when he came in, and a boggart may not pass through a closed door that has an iron lock in it, whether or not the key has been turned. The invasion of five more people, with their stomping feet and their cries and exclamations, was too much for the Boggart, and he uncoiled like a breaking spring and shot out of his hole – and, finding the door open, out into the corridor.

The door facing him at the end of the corridor was thick and ancient; it had no lock, but was held shut by a huge wooden bar set across it in two rests. In his rage, the Boggart lashed at the bar with a spell he had forgotten he knew, and it leaped out of the rests and crashed to the floor, leaving the great door to swing slowly open. In an instant the Boggart was through it – and high in the sun-warmed air, for this door was one of the safety barriers shutting off the ruined half of the castle, and beyond it was only a broken stone staircase ending in space.

The Boggart flickered crossly through the air,

twitching a tail feather from a passing seagull, which squawked resentfully. Then he dived down to the rocks to bother the seals.

In the library, the adults were at the far end of the room admiring Mr MacDevon's astrolabe, but Emily heard the crash of the falling bar through the beat of Jessup's music. She ran out into the corridor, dazzled by the bright light that now filled it – and gasped in terror as she skidded up against the fallen beam lying in her way. She would have toppled over it to the broken staircase below if Tommy, following, had not managed to grab her from behind.

He yelled angrily into the sky beyond her, 'You stupid idiot!' Dazed, Emily knew she was not the person he was yelling at, but she couldn't imagine who else it could be. Tommy let her go hastily, embarrassed to find himself still clutching her arm. He said, 'You all right?'

'Sure,' Emily said shakily. 'Thank you.'

It took the combined strength of Robert, Maggie, Mr Maconochie and all three children to get the wooden beam back in position, barring the perilous door. None of them actually spoke aloud their mind-shaking speculation over how on earth it could have been released in the first place. In their parents' pale startled faces, as they looked out at the gaping hole before the door closed it again, Emily and Jessup saw the end of any reluctance to sell Castle Keep.

'You can have one thing, to remind you,' Maggie said. 'One each. But it's got to be something that will go through the door at home.'

She was brisk in sweater, jeans and a kind of smock, looking like a dusty painter, with her hair tied back by a scarf, and a clipboard in her hand. In the company of Mr Maconochie, who seemed far more relaxed now in corduroys and an ancient sports jacket, she was touring the castle and choosing some of the more manageable pieces of furniture to be shipped to Toronto.

Emily said promptly, 'The little desk.'

In a corner of the MacDevon's library she had found a roll-top desk even more alluring than the one carried off by the dark impatient customer in her mother's shop.

Maggie laughed. 'I thought so. OK, it's yours. Jessup?'

'That table in our bedroom,' Jessup said. 'Under my computer it'll look *magnificent*.'

'But it's a washstand,' said Maggie. 'A

67

nineteenth-century washstand. It was meant to have a jug and a basin standing on it, in the days before bathrooms.'

'Well,' said Jessup placidly, 'now it's going to have a computer.'

Emily said, 'Can we put a few of the books into my desk?' She knew Mr Maconochie was arranging to have an Edinburgh bookseller come and inspect the contents of the MacDevon's library.

'Six, maximum. Packed so they won't bounce around.'

'All right!' said Emily happily.

The Boggart spent three days down on the seal rocks. Sometimes he would take the shape of a fish, and disappear just as a hungry seal tried to gulp him down; sometimes he would sit on the weed-covered rock and give an emerging seal just enough of a push to send it sliding back into the sea. He had an excellent time, and the seals, amiable, patient creatures, tolerated his antics with resignation. For them the Boggart was like the rocks or the ocean; he had always been there.

Satisfied, the Boggart flittered back into Castle Keep while everyone slept. In the pantry he helped himself to an orange, which he ate skin and all, and a hunk of cheese. He drank the top three inches from a carton of milk. He floated silently into the children's bedroom, where Emily and Jessup lay curled up in their sleeping bags at either side of an enormous four-poster bed, and he tied together the laces of Emily's trainers and hid all Jessup's socks in Emily's duffel bag. He loved the extra edge of being able to play tricks on two people at once, so that they could blame each other.

He ignored Maggie and Robert, since their door was closed, and with a sigh of home-coming contentment he flittered into the library. A silver bar of moonlight shone through one of the narrow windows and fell upon a book of poetry, lying on the open top of the roll-top desk. It was the last of the six books chosen by Emily and Jessup, which ranged from a centuries-old volume by King James I called *Daemonologie* to a sturdy *History of the Clans of the Western Highlands*, and it was full of Scottish ballads.

The Boggart was very partial to poetry, especially ballads. Over the years he had done a lot of reading, and even some tuneless private singing, in the library of the MacDevon family. He sat on the desk top, reading, entranced, until the shaft of moonlight moved sideways and fell away from the book, leaving it in the dark. Then suddenly he felt so agreeably tired that instead of flittering up to his usual high refuge, he crept into one of the inner compartments of the roll-top desk and fell asleep.

And so he was still there the next morning, sleeping soundly, when Emily came in and packed all six books in there with him, wedging them with crumpled newspaper, turning the iron key to lock them inside the desk to be shipped to Toronto.

CHAPTER FIVE

JESSUP WAS a founder member of the Gang of Five, a group of computer geeks. That was the phrase that had begun it, in an advertisement in the school's online newspaper: COMPUTER GEEKS UNITE! And then, in smaller letters: 'Anyone who lives in the Annex and is starved for intelligent conversation, contact jvhax3r online.'

The Annex was the area of Toronto in which the Volniks lived. jvhax3r had been Jessup, then aged nine, who had fallen in love with his father's computer at seven years old, inherited it at eight, and been communicating with it ever since in languages which none of his family could understand. He was said to have the IQ of a genius, but since this only showed itself in his mathematical relationship with the computer, nobody – including Jessup – paid it much attention. As far as Emily was concerned he was a normal pestiferous little brother, who happened to have some rather weird friends.

Two of these were gathered with Jessup now in his room, around his computer: Chris, a square, overweight eleven-year-old who in spite of his size was an amazingly agile goalie on Jessup's school ice hockey team, and Yung Hee, a small, exquisite and rather silent Korean-Canadian who at thirteen was already taking classes at the University of Toronto. The two other members of the Gang of Five were Raju, a slender twelve-year-old from Trinidad who had been carried off to England for a year by his academic parents, and Barry, a sixteen-year-old high school dropout from an alarmingly old and wealthy Toronto family. Barry described himself as a consultant auto mechanic, and was not welcome in the Volnik household because Maggie mistakenly suspected him of dealing drugs. 'He's too old for you,' she would say disapprovingly to Jessup. Emily's private opinion was that Barry looked permanently spaced-out not because he was stoned but because he was naturally weird. They all were, all the Gang of Five.

She stood in the open doorway, listening to the usual incomprehensible conversation.

'I rewrote the core rendering engine. It's shading just under three million polygons every ten milliseconds. And this is on my dad's old video card. It's smooth, when it doesn't crash.'

'Wow!'

'How'd you get to the code? I thought it was encrypted.'

'It was. The firmware has a backdoor.'

'Nice.'

It was a Friday evening, and Emily had just come home from her father's theatre. She had dropped in after school to see her friend Dai, the wardrobe master, who was deep in the designs for a production of Shakespeare's *Cymbeline* but had promised to dress Emily as a truly amazing vampire for Halloween. Though Halloween was still some way off, Emily was getting nervous.

'Jessup?' she said.

'Uh,' said her brother. His eyes were on the computer screen, and his fingers darting over its keyboard.

'Are you guys still doing Halloween?'

The Gang of Five had planned to dress up as characters from the new computer game they were designing. Emily's vampire was one of them too.

'Sure we are,' Chris said.

'D'you have costumes yet?'

'Don't worry about it, Em,' Jessup said, preoccupied. He pressed the keys, and a rocket shot across the screen and vaporized an asteroid.

'You don't have long.'

'My mom's doing them,' Chris said. He was staring at the screen too. 'That's control zero, Jess.'

'No, control three.'

'Really?'

'Control shift three,' Yung Hee said, in her soft musical voice.

Emily gave up, and went downstairs to feed the cat. This looked like being a night to send out for pizza. Maggie worked late at the shop every Friday, and at the theatre Emily had left her father besieged by people trying to solve the technical troubles of a new play set in the Arctic. Apparently the fake snow kept blowing from the stage into the auditorium, and making the audience sneeze. Robert would be home late again.

In the kitchen, small black Polly rubbed herself around Emily's legs, purring like a helicopter. There was a sudden ferocious bang at the front door, followed by the sound of the door opening and a cheerful shout. 'Em! Let's 'ave yer!' Emily put down the cat dish and grinned. That was Ron, one of the two drivers her mother hired whenever furniture had to be transported from house to shop, or shop to customer. He was large and cheery and newly immigrated from London, and nobody could understand more than half the things he said.

Ron loomed in the doorway, beaming at her, his muscles bulging out of a thin undershirt in spite of the cool air of October. 'Got some furniture for you, me love! Straight from Scotland – full a' porridge, by the feel of it!'

'*Oh!*' said Emily. Everyday life swallowed them so completely since they came back from Scotland that she had forgotten all about the furniture from Castle Keep – and even the castle itself. She had sent Tommy a postcard of Toronto the day after they came home, and he had sent her one with a picture of a seal, which was pinned up on her noticeboard between a Wilderness Society sticker and an old photograph of Jessup and herself throwing snow at each other, laughing. But Appin seemed another world, distant and magical and different. Suddenly now it blossomed in her mind, the grey sea and misted mountains, and the dark romantic shape of Castle Keep, and she was filled with excitement that a real piece of it would soon be in her room.

The members of the Gang of Five begrudgingly paused in the development of their computer game while Ron and his equally large friend Jim steered Jessup's Scottish table – or washstand – up the narrow stairs to the third floor.

'Up the apples!' sang Ron. 'Mind y'backs, boys!' He hoisted the table over the banister.

'Apples?' said Chris.

'Apples and pears,' Emily said promptly. 'That means stairs. It rhymes. Use your loaf.'

Chris stared at her. Emily giggled. She and Jessup had adopted Ron's Cockney rhyming slang with such delight, when their mother first hired him, that Robert had starting fining them five cents for every unintelligible word used in family conversations.

'Loaf means loaf of bread. Which means head.'

'Gobbledegook,' Chris said.

'Speak for yourself,' said Emily. 'How do you think your computer talk sounds to normal people?'

'All right, Em, me old china,' said Ron. 'Where d'you want the desk?'

'In here!' She ran eagerly to clear a space in her bedroom, while the two big men clattered down the stairs. They came back in an oddly erratic course, rocking from side to side of the staircase.

'Watch it, Jim!'

'Keep it steady, then!'

'*Whoops* –' Ron grabbed one corner of the desk as it threatened to gouge a hole in the wall. 'Gorblimey,' he said. 'Talk about the end of a perfect day! It's been crazy, bringing this stuff over. Traffic lights going dead, cars stopping right under our wheels – never known nothin' like it. Thank Gawd this one's the last.' He dropped his end of the desk – and Jim roared, as it lurched sideways on to his foot.

'Stone me,' said Ron in disgust. 'It's bewitched. Sorry, mate.'

They left, muttering, and Emily surveyed her desk proudly. It looked very pretty, set between the tall bookcase and the door opposite her bed. She unhooked the little key that had been hanging all this time from a drawing pin on her notice-board, above Tommy's postcard, and she unlocked the desk and rolled back its graceful wooden top.

And the Boggart, who had slept for two months and woken to find himself in a small dark space surrounded by lurching books, came flittering resentfully out into the air of Canada.

*

Jessup stared in pained astonishment at the paper tray on the kitchen table. 'Who took the last slice of pizza?'

'Not me,' said Emily.

'Not me,' said Chris with his mouth full.

Emily took a swig from her glass of milk. 'It was you, Jess. The computer's sucked out your brain.'

'But it was there a second ago,' Jessup said. He looked up from the tray, confused. 'Wasn't it?'

The Boggart sat on the shelf above the gas stove, among the pots and pans, chewing ecstatically. What was this wonderful, extraordinary new dish? He had always loved cheese, but this was delicious beyond belief, a quintessence of cheese. And mingled with it were several other alluring tastes, savoury, delectable. His horrified resentment of the strange new world in which he found himself began to change into a cautious wondering.

He finished the stolen piece of pizza, looked around unsuccessfully for more, and flittered down to drink from Emily's glass of milk. This was an extra treat; the MacDevon had drunk only tea, which the Boggart found uninteresting.

Emily stomped on the pizza box and thrust it into the recycling bin. Turning back to the table, she saw her glass, now empty. She stared for a moment, then looked at Jessup. 'Oh, very funny,' she said.

'What's funny?'

'I'm supposed to say, *Who drank the rest of my milk?* – so you can say *Not me.*'

'I should think I would,' said Jessup with energy. 'Drink *your* milk? Yuck! What a disgusting idea.'

Emily looked uncertainly from him to Chris to the empty glass, and hesitated. Up on his shelf, the Boggart chuckled silently to himself.

'Ice cream,' Jessup said briskly. He went to the refrigerator and opened the freezer compartment, standing on tiptoe to peer in. 'There's vanilla, chocolate or butter crunch. Chris?'

The Boggart's eyes grew round.

Chris said hopefully, 'Got any fudge sauce?'

Jessup opened the main door of the refrigerator, took out a jar and handed it wordlessly to Emily. Chris beamed. 'Vanilla, please,' he said.

'And chocolate for Em, and butter crunch for me.'

Jessup withdrew from the freezer with an armful of large ice-cream tubs. Emily unscrewed the cap of the fudge sauce jar, set the jar in the microwave oven and punched several buttons. The microwave produced a humming whir for a little while, ending with a loud chirrup and three bleeps, and the

Boggart's eyes grew rounder still. By the time he saw three dishes of ice cream put on the table, all different colours, with shining dark sauce topping each like a glossy hat, his mouth was watering so hard it was all he could do not to snatch one of the dishes out of Jessup's hand. Instead, while they were all busy eating, he flittered down and stole the fudge sauce jar, which still had an inch or so of sauce inside. He was about to help himself to a handful of ice cream as well when Emily suddenly noticed that the three tubs were still there on the table, in the warm room, and she whisked them back into the freezer.

The Boggart watched sadly as they disappeared. He had seen a refrigerator before, in the Camerons' store; he knew it to be a box with a metal door, which no boggart could open. But the first taste of the fudge sauce sent all longing memories of ice cream right out of his head. What was *this*? The smooth chocolatey sweetness was like an explosion of delight in his mouth. He ate by putting his small hand into the jar and scooping up a little at a time, slowly, happily, licking the sticky dark sauce lingeringly off each long finger. He was in love. He had forgotten all about Castle Keep. The astounding luscious taste of fudge sauce made him feel that this odd new world in which he found himself just might be heaven.

Emily said, 'I don't *believe* this. Where's the jar of fudge sauce gone?'

The Boggart began his tricks gently. Over his centuries of mischief, he had learned not to rush things. The temptation was, of course, to dive into someone's life like a puppy running rampage in a tidy room; to turn everything upside down, all at once, in a great gleeful eruption of trickery. But that was like gobbling a whole bag of sweets in five minutes. In the long run, there was much more fun to be had by taking your time.

So in a leisurely, temperate way, he started by hiding things. Robert left his razor on the bathroom windowsill as usual after his morning shave, came back next morning and reached for it sleepily – and found it gone. He turned the whole bathroom upside down in a furious unsuccessful search, and only when he was frustrated, cross and late for an appointment did Maggie come across the razor quite by accident in the bedroom.

Where did you find it?

On your bedside table.

What the hell was it doing there?

I guess you put it there, honey . . .

And the Boggart sat there listening, smiling. He would not play another trick on Robert until he had similarly removed Emily's algebra book from her bedroom desk to the kitchen vegetable rack, Maggie's favourite hat from the hall coat rack to the upstairs linen cupboard, and Jessup's hockey stick to the basement laundry room. And in a careful patterning these tricks would be interspersed with others.

For instance, the Boggart enjoyed moving a chair or a lamp two feet away from its customary place, so that it had to be moved back, usually by Robert, with muttered threats against the life of the once-a-week cleaning lady. If Emily tidied a bedroom drawer, the Boggart jumbled things up again. When Jessup organized all the books on his shelves alphabetically, by subject and author, the Boggart moved them into a different order overnight – using what he felt was an artistic pattern, with all the vowels lumped together in the middle of the alphabet. And when Maggie filled the sugar bowl with sugar one day, she found next morning that it was full of salt. The discovery was rather noisy, since Robert had just put a heaped spoonful into his breakfast coffee, stirred it briskly and taken a large gulp.

The family reacted to all this in a satisfyingly predictable manner. At first each of them blamed himself or herself, for absent-mindedness. *How could I have been dumb enough to leave that there?* they would think, helplessly. But after a while they began privately to suspect that the absent-mindedness belonged to someone else. *It was Maggie who moved my razor, but she's forgotten.* Slowly this became a mutual irritation, and as the Boggart's tricks became progressively more obvious, it grew into a conviction, in everyone's separate mind, that some other member of the family was deliberately playing practical jokes.

Em, I wish you'd stop changing the books on my shelves. It's not funny.

I haven't touched your books.

You must have – who else would do it?

The Boggart hugged himself as he listened to the spurts and flares of impatience. This was the first part of the game, the prelude. This beginning time was his private pleasure, the time in which only he knew what was really happening. Very soon they would all move to the next: to the moment when he would push them over the edge, into the delicious discovery of the real inventor of all the tricks and jokes. After that there would come a different pleasure; they would realize that they had a boggart in the house, and live with him according to the time-honoured rules. He would keep them from becoming bored; they would, on the whole, enjoy him. And he would be part of the family, like a quirky but valued relative. Just as he had been for so long with the MacDevon.

It's just you, is it then, my mannie? I'll be after you one of these days . . .

So the Boggart looked ahead in happy anticipation, not knowing that he was living now in a world which no longer believed in boggarts, a world which had driven out the Old Things and buried the Wild Magic deep under layers of reason and time.

CHAPTER SIX

THE BOGGART'S tricks were not daily events. He had no interest in trying out a joke unless he was fairly sure he would find it funny, so days would go by in which he did no mischief, but only explored – still cautiously – the place in which he now lived. He also rested, in his usual erratic pattern, with infrequent but long periods of sleep. In Emily's bedroom he had found the shelf on which four of the books from the MacDevon's library now stood. (The other two, *Daemonologie* and the book about the clans, were in Jessup's room.) She had put them in a place of honour, set apart from the other books, propped between two heavy brass vases which served as bookends.

Susan Cooper

Inside one of the vases, on a bed of cotton-wool balls stolen from the bathroom, the Boggart slept. Once in a while, roused by formless dreams in which he heard the waves lapping on Loch Linnhe, or the distant bark of a seal, he would reach a long arm out of the case and touch, for comfort, the cover of the book of Scottish ballads from Castle Keep.

The kitten Polydore discovered him in his brass vase not long after he chose it as his bed. She was a house cat now, not allowed outdoors for fear of traffic and the other perils of city streets, so she spent her time checking up on every smallest corner of the Volnik house. She toured every room, every day, leaping up on to bookshelves and chests and bureaux, stepping delicately around ornaments and photograph frames. And brass vases used as bookends.

The day she found the Boggart, he was asleep. He woke to find Polly's head filling the top of his vase, and he reached up crossly and gave her whiskers a violent tweak. Polly yowled, jumped backwards, and fell off the bookcase. She gave the Boggart's vase a wide berth after that, but the Boggart occasionally amused himself by drinking her milk from one side of the saucer while she

86

lapped it from the other, or dropping spiky unexpected objects into her cat bed just as she prepared to lie down.

Polly didn't know what to make of him; her life had never contained an invisible nuisance before. Whenever she sensed that he was near her she would crouch warily in a corner, with her ears pricked. The family began to notice this after a while, and decided with regret that their cat, though lovable, must also be a little crazy.

After the sheltered life he had led for so long in Castle Keep, the Boggart was at first baffled by the Volnik house. In Scotland he had never encountered anything electrical except the lights, telephone and radio in the Camerons' shop, since the MacDevon had always flatly refused to have electricity in the castle. The first time the Boggart saw Maggie switching on the television set, to produce a bright flickering image of a small world inside a box, he was astounded. Clearly Maggie, like himself, could work magic.

This was confirmed when he saw Maggie in the kitchen, with a magical whirring whisk that beat eggs all on its own at her command, and a magic kettle that boiled water without being set on the stove. Even when she cleaned her teeth in the bathroom, she had a toothbrush whose bristles magically buzzed up and down while her hand remained still. Maggie Volnik, the Boggart decided, must be a witch. It took him several days to realize that everyone else around him was capable of the same magic simply by pressing a switch that brought electric current out of a wire.

After that, electricity became a challenge. The Boggart had to see whether this amazing strange power could be mastered by his own magic. Sure enough, it could. After a little practice, he could hover behind Maggie in the kitchen and make her electric beater stop and go backwards, producing some gratifying splashing and shrieks. He could make the lights flicker as if a bulb were about to burn out, or make the telephone ring even though nobody was calling. Soon he found he could also change the channel on the screen of the television set. The day he first tried was a Saturday. Jessup was watching a hockey game, and Emily was sitting at the table drawing a map of Greece for her homework.

Jessup howled suddenly. 'Em! Put it back!'

Emily looked up. 'Put what back?'

'The game! C'mon, it's the third period!'

'Are you crazy? I haven't done a thing.'

'Oh big joke, I know you've got the remote. Come *on*, I was watching the Maple Leafs and the Bruins and now I've got some old woman making a cake.'

Jessup dived at the television set, without noticing the remote control lying peacefully at its side, and he changed the channel – and found the cooking programme facing him on every channel he turned to. He swung vengefully around and launched himself at Emily, who threw her book at him in self-defence.

'I don't *have* the remote!' she yelled.

The Boggart chuckled joyously, and Polly the kitten hissed at him from underneath the armchair. He took care not to repeat the same trick often. Instead he tried others, like turning the television set off into silent darkness at the climax of a thriller, or turning it on in the middle of the night. Robert called in a television repairman, who charged him ninety-five dollars and told him there was nothing wrong with the set.

Robert was not seen often at home at the moment, since he was not only running his theatre but directing its next production, *Cymbeline*. Maggie was coping with the arrival of her second shipment of furniture from Castle Keep, Emily was organizing a recycling drive at school, and Jessup was neglecting his computer and the Gang of Five for the sake of hockey practice. They all met at brisk intervals for breakfast and dinner.

One breakfast time, Emily was filling lunch boxes. 'Jess? You want peanut butter and jam again?'

'Of course!'

'Gross!' said Emily to herself in quiet revulsion, as she dug the knife deep into the peanut-butter jar. The Boggart sat on the table, watching hungrily. He had discovered that he loved peanut butter, but never found himself in control of all the makings for the peanut-butter-and-jam sandwich that went, every day without fail, into Jessup's lunch box. Watching Emily slather chunky peanut butter on one piece of bread, and glistening blackberry jam on the other, he was filled with such greed that he decided he must, he absolutely must, get to this sandwich before Jessup did. So when Emily fitted the sandwich, inside its neat plastic bag, into the lunch box along with the thermos, the cookies and the apple, the Boggart slipped in with it.

Emily closed the box, and Jessup seized it as he rushed past her with his sports bag. 'Cat's acting crazy again,' he said. 'Thanks, Em. Bye.'

Emily saw Polly the cat hunched in a corner of the room, taut and nervous – but as Jessup disappeared towards the front door, Polly instantly relaxed and strolled over towards the table, purring hopefully. Emily frowned. Was the cat afraid of Jessup? The cat *adored* Jessup. It didn't make any sense – like a lot of things that had been happening in the Volnik house recently.

The Boggart bounced up and down in the lunch box as Jessup ran to school. He clung to a hinge, fending off the apple with his feet, listening to the strange roaring sounds that were first the noise of traffic, and afterwards the shouting of many ten-year-olds. Like all boggarts, he could alter his size and shape as he chose. But it was uncomfortable to stay at a forced size for more than an hour or two, and by the time Jessup opened his box at lunchtime the Boggart was decidedly stiff and cramped.

But that hadn't stopped him from eating Jessup's sandwich. Once the lunch box had stopped its bouncing, after being safely stowed in Jessup's locker, the Boggart had pulled open the plastic bag and settled himself down to chomp happily through the sticky meld of jam, peanut butter and bread.

Now he was full and sleepy, and the plastic bag held nothing but crumbs. Jessup stared at them in outrage at lunchtime when he opened the box.

'Somebody stole my sandwich!'

'Musta been disappointed,' said Chris placidly, opening his own. 'You had peanut butter again, huh?'

'It was locked up! Someone must know my locker combination!'

'Let's go get a taco. You got any money?'

'Some,' said Jessup guardedly.

'Come on then.' Chris jumped up. There was a little Tex-Mex café a block from the school which did a thriving business with sandwich-spurning children at lunchtimes.

'But it's pocket money! I'm not spending my pocket money on *lunch*!'

Chris sat down again. He said reluctantly, 'You better have half my sandwich, then.'

'What is it?'

'Spam.'

'Yuck,' said Jessup ungratefully.

'Well, take your pick, man. Spam or bucks.'

Jessup had no trouble with the choice. His pocket money was earmarked for computer games. They sat morosely eating Chris' sandwich, and

Jessup gave Chris half his cookies, to make up. The Boggart hovered at their elbows, stealing any chocolate chips that fell out of the cookies. He found the school an alarming place – so many children, all at once! – and when lunch was over he draped himself over Jessup's shoulder, for safety, with one leg tucked inside the collar of Jessup's sweatshirt. This gave Jessup a slight itch, and he reached up half-consciously to scratch his neck from time to time. The Boggart would have liked to sleep, but he had to keep a wary eye open for the hand coming towards him, and dodge.

He sat there all through a history lesson about the Roman Empire, which – having lived in the Roman Empire, for the four hundred years during which it had included the British Isles – he found inaccurate and boring. After that he clung desperately to the sweatshirt collar while Jessup raced through the school with Chris to get to hockey practice. In the changing room the Boggart hovered nervously in the air as the team changed, ducking when they threw pads at each other, puzzling over the fact that boys so young should be putting on the kind of protective padding only worn, in his own experience, by medieval knights practising for a joust.

But once he was out on the hockey rink, sheltering breathless inside Jessup's face mask as he whizzed over the ice, he realized that nothing had changed. This *was* a joust. It was just as passionate and just as dangerous, even though conducted by children. Admittedly they were whacking with their weapons not at each other, at least not often, but at the small rounded black object they seemed to call a puck. (Some old dark sorcery at work there, the Boggart thought suspiciously – why else call your victim by one of the names of the most ancient good spirit of all?) But they were certainly preparing for a major contest, all of them battling to be thought worthy of competing in the tournament.

He was so deep in these reflections, sitting on Jessup's shoulder while Jessup waited on the bench, that he was taken by surprise when a shout from the coach whirled the next forward line out on to the ice. Jessup dived into the game so fast that the Boggart had no time to shelter inside his face mask; he grabbed one of its bars from the outside and hung on, desperately dangling. Far down the ice a defence player hit the puck, and it rose up and flew towards Jessup. Caught off balance, Jessup could only dodge sideways, so that the puck narrowly missed his helmet. It hit the Boggart instead.

Nobody was ever able to report precisely what happened: the details were too fast for a human eye to see. The puck disappeared, vaporized by contact with the power of the Old Magic; but the Boggart, jolted by the impact even though boggarts cannot be hurt or feel pain, became suddenly visible. Curled up into a small, dense shape, he shot across the ice – looking just like a hockey puck. And the same defence player, an aggressive dark-haired boy called Pete Defarge, swung back his stick joyously and hit him high into the air.

The Boggart-puck hurtled over the heads of the teams – but instead of falling down again, it flew on. Making a strange whistling sound, it wheeled high into the stadium, flying in circles, faster and faster, around and around. The players stood frozen on the ice, looking up; the coach and umpires and substitutes gaped from the sidelines. Furious, manic, the Boggart wheeled once more – and disappeared. The stadium was silent, as everyone waited for the sound of the puck falling, and heard nothing.

Coach Bonhomme, who had felt a strange cold terror while he watched, suddenly found his voice. 'OK, what are you waiting for?' He threw another puck on to the ice. 'Let's go, boys – Volnik, Passant, play ball!'

As if wakened from a dream, the players began moving again, first slowly, then faster, as the game took on its own new momentum. Every boy on the ice was trying to forget, to pretend that he had not seen what he had seen – how could a hockey puck fly in circles, *whistling*? So they played even more furiously than before, as if they were opposing not their own classmates but some hated rival team. Chris leaped about in his goal behind his pads; Jessup and the other forwards flickered like lightning over the rink, and the defence players crashed about, skidding. It was fast efficient hockey until the moment when Jessup whirled down the ice with the puck, with Pete Defarge dashing at him for a tackle – and suddenly with all the speed and power of the Wild Magic the Boggart was back, diving vengefully between the two, tipping Defarge sideways so ferociously that he seemed to turn a cartwheel. His stick snapped in two, his arms and legs whirled; he hurtled on his back across the ice and his helmeted head crashed against the wall.

Pete Defarge lay still. And in the instant before rushing to pick him up, everyone glanced reproachfully at Jessup, who seemed to have tripped him deliberately with a vicious foul play.

*

'But I didn't!' Jessup said indistinctly, through his mouth guard.

'He's not hurt,' Coach Bonhomme said. 'Fortunately.'

'Coach, I didn't trip him! I was just coming up the ice, I didn't have time!'

Coach Bonhomme sighed. He was a burly man with a flattened nose, an ex-professional who had seen every dirty trick that can be played on a hockey rink, and had indeed played most of them. He said, 'I saw you, Volnik. Seein's believin'.'

Jessup pulled off his helmet and spat out the mouth guard. 'You saw the puck go up in the air and fly around the rink three times too – did you believe that?'

Coach Bonhomme shrugged. 'Seein's believin',' he said again. 'Sure I did. Didn't you?'

CHAPTER SEVEN

J ESSUP SPENT all his next hockey game on the bench, as a punishment for illegally tripping Pete Defarge. He was cross. Nobody, not even his friends, really seemed to believe that he hadn't done it. They believed he hadn't *intended* to, but like Coach Bonhomme, they couldn't get past the evidence of their own eyes. Or in his parents' case, the evidence of so many other eyes. 'Never mind,' they said forgivingly, infuriatingly, to Jessup. 'You didn't mean to hurt him. It was an accident.'

The only person who was sympathetic, to his surprise, was Emily.

'Grown-ups can be so dumb,' she said. 'If you know you didn't do it, then of course you didn't.'

'But who did?'

'Maybe Pete tripped.'

'No way. One minute he was coming towards me, and the next he was flying in the other direction. I mean *flying.*'

'Weird,' Emily said, shaking her head. 'Like the TV, and the lights flickering, and stuff. I was telling Nat about that today. She said maybe it was sunspots.' Nat was Natalie, her closest friend at school, who was a serious astronomer and on fine winter nights spent hours of after-school time looking through her telescope.

'Emily! Jessup!' It was Maggie calling them to supper. They ran, and the Boggart breathed an impatient sigh of relief. He had been waiting for them to get out of Jessup's room so that he could leave a surprise present there.

Since the hockey game, the Boggart had been feeling guilty. It was an emotion he had never felt before, and he found it very uncomfortable. But he knew he had given Jessup a bad time, in ways he hadn't intended. Robbing his lunch box was one thing – getting him labelled as a cheat and a liar was far more serious. What's more, he, the Boggart, had broken his own rules: he had attacked Pete Defarge on the ice not for fun but for furious revenge. The laws of the Wild Magic allowed this as a defence against evil and murder, but not against an accidental whack from a hockey puck.

So the Boggart wanted to do something nice for Jessup. He had thought back over all his brief experience to find the thing that seemed to give Jessup the most pleasure, and he felt he had found the answer. He had made him a peanut-butter-and-jam sandwich.

It wasn't a very elegant sandwich, because it had been done in a hurry, during the few hasty minutes when Emily was filling the lunch boxes that day. Hovering close and invisible over Emily's hands, and flickering fast through the air like a mad hummingbird, the Boggart had managed to grab two slices of wholemeal bread, a big handful of peanut butter and a handful of jam. He had then put them all together as fast as he could, before the jam leaked through his fingers or the bread – very healthy, but very crumbly – fell apart. Then he flittered off to Jessup's bedroom, carrying a sandwich which looked rather like the planet Saturn surrounded by its rings: a golf-ball-sized glob of peanut butter encased in bread, with a rim of bread crust out of which red jam oozed like thick blood.

He put the sandwich down now, with a sigh of relief – and some regret, since the smell of peanut butter was making him ravenous. Before he could be tempted to eat it, he flittered out of Jessup's room and back to his brass-vase refuge on Emily's bookshelf. Good deeds were very tiring, though surprisingly satisfying, and he needed a rest. He curled up on his bed of cotton-wool balls, smiling contentedly, for perhaps a three-day sleep.

And Jessup came running upstairs after supper to chat online with the other members of the Gang of Five, and without switching on his bedroom light he settled himself happily down to wake up his computer.

Then he yelled, and slowly and stickily, he stood up.

The Boggart had carefully left his gift in the place where he felt Jessup was most likely to see it – his computer chair.

Tommy sent Emily another postcard. The picture showed a small island called Staffa, with strange dark cliffs like carvings. The postcard said, 'Staffa is seven miles away and Mendelssohn composed *Fingal's Cave* there. Life here is uninteresting but there is snow on the hills. The castle is empty and no one comes to see it. I hope you and Jessup are well. Yours sincerely, Tommy.'

Emily stuck the postcard up on her noticeboard next to the seal and James Dean, and went to the music store, which was rocking to the beat of the Red Hot Chili Peppers, to investigate the music of Mendelssohn. One of the clerks had never heard of him, a second said vaguely, 'Classical – upstairs,' and a third said, 'Of course – his *Hebrides Overture*,' and found her a CD. He was a husky young man wearing a vintage T-shirt emblazoned SAVE THE DOLPHINS. This endeared him to Emily, who felt passionately about endangered species and wanted to save everything.

'Nice piece,' said the young man amiably. 'You know it?'

'Not yet,' said Emily.

He smiled at her as he handed over her change. 'See if you can find the words inside it. They aren't there but you can hear them. They say, "How lovely the sea is!"'

Emily went home and played the CD, and instantly heard the words in the tune – even though, as the young man had said, there were really no words there. She sat for a while thinking about this, looking vacantly at Tommy's postcard. Then she wrote back to him, on a postcard showing a picture of a Canadian pine forest.

'This is a painting by Emily Carr,' she wrote. 'I am named after her. Our castle furniture has come. I am going to be a vampire for Halloween. Jessup and I are very well. Yours sincerely, Emily.'

Then she scribbled at the bottom, in small hasty letters, 'Weird things are happening here, like the words in *Fingal's Cave* that aren't really there.'

Late on the afternoon of Halloween, Emily stopped at the theatre hoping that Dai might have had time to finish her costume. She was half expecting not to get one, since Robert had given her a chilly lecture at breakfast about bothering busy professionals in the crucial time just before a play opens. He had said a number of other things too that she was trying to forget. The blame for Jessup's peanut-buttered trousers had landed squarely on Emily, in spite of all her denials. Who else in the family could possibly have booby-trapped Jessup's chair?

But Dai was waiting for her, and he had outdone himself. He dressed Emily in black tights, and a close-fitting long-sleeved black top with black sequins glued all over it. On her feet he put soft leather boots that seemed black in the daylight, but in the dark glowed spookily with an awful greenish light. A sweeping black cloak went over everything, and its lining glowed with the same green fluorescence. Dai shut Emily briefly in a dark room so that she could see it, and she was happily terrified.

'How does it *do* that?' she demanded.

'Trade secret, darling,' said Dai. He was a small brown-faced man of indeterminate age, originally from Wales, with dark curly hair. 'Shut up now and open your mouth.'

Emily obeyed, and he fitted a magnificent vampire fang over each of her two top canine teeth. They curved out and down over her lower lip, looking alarmingly real. 'Just a touch of glue,' Dai said. 'They'll stay on for about three hours, if you're careful. Course, you won't be able to eat, but you could always suck blood.' He winked at her.

'I look terrible,' Emily said contentedly, leering at the mirror.

'Last touch,' Dai said, and over her blonde hair he fitted an unnerving black wig made not from hair but from long black velvet ribbons. Emily tossed her head, watching the mirror, and giggled. 'Awesome!'

'And if you want to dribble some nice bright blood, you bite on this.' He handed her a capsule that looked like a large vitamin pill. 'Coming to the party, then?'

Louise Spring the general manager, owner of Fred the dog, gave a famous party every Halloween, to which the working members of the Chervil company came very late, after their performance. Sometimes Emily and Jessup were allowed to spend a sleepy hour there before bed. Not this year.

Emily's spirits dropped, as she remembered her father's cold lecture of the morning. 'No. We're grounded. We can't even go trick-or-treating, we have to just be home in our costumes and open the door to other kids.'

Dai clicked his tongue in friendly concern. 'Poor babies. What's Dragon-Daddy mad about?'

Emily smiled mournfully. She had discovered only recently that when Robert was in a rage, he was known to the company, behind his back, as Dragon-Daddy. But the smile drooped into gloom under Dai's sympathetic gaze, and suddenly she found herself telling him all about the sandwich mishap, and Jessup's hockey problem, and the flying hockey puck and the erratic television and Polly's odd behaviour, and all the other peculiar things that had begun creeping into the life of the

Volnik family. The words all came out with a slight lisp, because Emily had to talk past the vampire teeth.

She was in mid-flow when the door opened, and a large new presence was filling the room: an elderly man with a very round face and a deep, resonant voice. 'Sorry I'm late, dear boy. I have lunched well – too well, perhaps –' He caught sight of Emily, and lurched backwards in exaggerated terror. 'Angels and ministers of grace defend us! A vampire!'

'Hi, Willie,' said Emily. William Walker was the senior actor in her father's company; not the best, but the most permanent. He was a genial, talkative man who played venerable dukes in Shakespeare, and elderly character parts in everything else, and though he would never be a Lear or a Falstaff everybody loved him. So did Robert, even when he mocked Willie's plummy English diction, which took on a noticeable Scottish burr whenever he had had one drink too many.

Willie took Emily's hand and turned her in a circle, inspecting her. 'Stupendous,' he said to Dai, in warm congratulation. The two of them shared a house on the edge of a Toronto ravine, and had three cats.

Dai was frowning. 'She had a problem you should hear about,' he said. He made Emily repeat her story, in every detail. As she finished, trying unsuccessfully not to lisp, she saw them looking thoughtfully at each other. Dai raised his eyebrows in some private enquiry; Willie nodded, slowly.

'It's a boggart,' Willie said.

'That's what I was thinking,' said Dai.

'What?' said Emily.

'Something they don't teach you in school,' Dai said. He hesitated; then went on in a rush. 'He's a spirit, like. Lives in a family, and plays tricks. The Scots call him a boggart. In Wales we call him a *pwca*. Dunno what the English call him – maybe they have dogs instead.' He chuckled to himself. Dai had once been a Welsh Nationalist, and liked to be rude to any members of the company who had English blood. He added regretfully, 'I've never run into one. Willie has, though. Twice.'

'I could have done without it,' Willie said.

Emily said slowly, 'You mean a ghost?'

'No – a spirit,' Willie said. He sounded suddenly much more Scottish than usual. 'Not something left over from a dead person. A boggart's a person himself – just not human. And you can't see him or hear him, not unless he wants you to. He's not a bad fellow, he's like a kid, really. Wants to have fun. I never heard of one this side of the ocean, though.'

'Nor did I,' Dai said. He looked at Emily oddly. 'What did you bring back from that Scottish trip of yours, Em?'

'If you two are putting me on, I wish you wouldn't,' Emily said uneasily.

Willy flashed a sudden smile at her. The light bulb was behind him, turning the remaining hair on his bald head into a glowing halo. He clapped his hands, and it was like a release. 'Go off trick-or-treating, Mistress Vampire,' he said. 'Have a good time.'

Emily jumped up, relieved, and gave them a fang-toothed grin. 'Thanks for the costume, Dai. Happy Halloween!'

Willy said casually, 'But if you have any more trouble, come back and tell me, OK?'

'I will,' Emily said.

Four of the members of the Gang of Five were waiting for Emily at the Volniks' house, dressed as characters from their new computer game. This game, which was called Black Hole, was in a constant state of development; the Gang never seemed to finish it, because one or other of them was always having a new idea. It was all about spaceships which discovered numbers of different worlds while trying to avoid being dragged through black holes in space. Emily's vampire came from one of these worlds, and so did the spiderlike creature represented by Chris's costume, which had a round black body fitted over his head and most of his own body, and six extra legs the same size and shape as his own. He scuttled down the pavement to meet Emily, looking hideously lifelike with all eight legs moving at once.

'Terrific!' said Emily, baring her fangs at him. The spider gave a muffled squeak, and backed away, narrowly missing a seven-foot shiny rocket with flame-coloured legs, which was standing at a rather drunken angle beside the front door.

'Hey, babe,' said Barry's voice hollowly from inside the rocket. 'Nice teeth.'

'Nice legs,' said Emily. 'Dad should put you in *Cymbeline.*'

'Your father's not in a great mood,' said the rocket bleakly.

'Emily, you look wonderful!' It was Yung Hee's soft voice, from a floating ghostly form draped in several different shades of yellow, orange and red chiffon. She was Fire Burst, one of the dire fates that could overcome a player in the game of Black Hole. Beside her was Jessup, his head, hands and legs sticking out of a white cube of polystyrene supposed to represent Ice Death, another hazard. By the time the Gang's Halloween plans had reached the design of Ice Death, their inventiveness had started to run down.

'So what's up with Dad?' said Emily to Jessup.

Two very small ghosts in white sheets came along the street and paused, giggling nervously. One of them saw Chris in his spider costume and darted back to clutch its mother's hand.

'Crazy things happening,' Jessup said. 'Tell you later. He's gone to the theatre.' He picked up a basket of sweets and stalked over to the ghosts and their mother.

Yung Hee came close to Emily and spoke into her ear. She said, 'You know that carved-out pumpkin you had on the doorstep? Your father came out of the door and it smashed on the ground right in front of him, spattered bits of pumpkin guck all over his jacket. He yelled at Jessup for throwing it at him – but I *saw*, Jessup and I were right here in front of the house. And we saw that pumpkin jump up in the air and smash itself down on the concrete. We did, Em, truly. *It jumped!'*

The Boggart had woken only two hours before, on his cotton-wool bed in the vase on Emily's shelf. He stretched, and gave a large happy yawn. He wondered why he felt so cheerful, and then remembered his good deed, the gift of Jessup's peanut-butter-and-jam sandwich. The cheerfulness was a pleasant surprise, though the good deed had involved so much effort that he didn't especially want to repeat it. He flittered up out of the vase and sat on the edge of the bookshelf.

The daylight was beginning to die, at this time of the year when the sun went down at about four in the afternoon. Outside the window a half-moon hung in the sky, which was tinged a strange pinkish violet after the sunset. A small sudden wind shifted the top shoots of the tall holly bush that grew beside the house – a bush very rare in winter-frigid Toronto, and much cherished by Robert. The Boggart stiffened, as if he were hearing a warning sound, and all at once he realized what day would dawn tomorrow. *Samhain!*

The Boggart still clung to the oldest beliefs about the shape of the year, Celtic beliefs that had been in his head for two thousand years and more. For him, Halloween was not All Hallows Eve but the ancient Eve of Samhain, the marker between summer and winter. From that night on, the world was ruled all through the winter by the skinny blue-faced hag, the Cailleach Bheur. All summer long the Cailleach Bheur had been shut up inside a stone, a grey stone lying under a holly tree. But on the Eve of Samhain she sprang up out of the stone, with her black eyes glittering like cold pebbles in her pinched blue face, and she seized her staff and went about the countryside striking at the earth, to kill all green growth. Her breath frosted the windows and set icicles on branches and the corners of roofs, and when she sang her terrible winter song into the sky, the words froze into snowflakes and whirled down to cover the bare trees and mound deep drifts against houses and barns.

The red-berried holly was one of the few plants to survive unchanged through her icy dominion, and so people would set branches of holly over their doors and windows and mantels, to persuade her to stay out. And on their doorsteps they left harvest offerings of vegetables and fruit, so that she would eat there, instead of storming into their kitchens in a whirl of hail and snow.

The Boggart was alarmed. Now it was the Eve of Samhain once more, and the Cailleach Bheur would be out roaming the world, and nobody in this house had done anything to protect it against her wrath. Her wrinkled blue face would be at the window soon, her cold breath blowing down the chimney. In a panic the Boggart flittered downstairs and out through the part-open front door. He quivered as he saw strange creatures standing out there, surely part of the wild retinue of the Cailleach Bheur; but then his sense told him that they were only Jessup and his friends.

He saw with relief that they had at least left out a pumpkin on the step, as an offering – but it was not chopped up small as it properly should be, for the winter hag's toothless jaws. He dived down and snatched up the pumpkin, and hastily dropped it on the step, smashing it into small pieces, ignoring the tiresome interruption of Robert Volnik, who chose that moment to come out the front door.

Then he flittered back indoors, to find other ways of defending the house against the rage of the blue-faced Cailleach Bheur, and so he missed the sound of Robert's pumpkin-spattered rage, and the arrival of Emily with her vampire teeth.

*

The creatures of the Black Hole failed to notice the Boggart's comings and goings; they were too busy scaring trick-or-treaters. In theory they – or at any rate Emily and Jessup – were restricted to spending the evening meekly inside the front door, waiting to answer the doorbell and hand out sweets to more fortunate, mobile children. But in the absence of his parents Jessup, with the help of the Gang, had no intention of behaving so passively. If he wasn't allowed to go out collecting sweets, he was at least going to make sure he didn't have to give any away.

So in the dark street outside the house, Chris the spider patrolled the pavement, in short scuttling dashes that sent the smallest trick-or-treaters shrieking away to a less alarming front door. For any older and more intrepid visitors who got as far as the front path, Jessup the Ice Death lurched to and fro uttering short awful noises like a kind of mechanical belch; Yung Hee the Fire Burst floated half-visible in the darkness beside the house, moaning softly and heartrendingly as if she were in great pain, and Barry, lurking behind a crab-apple tree, filled his silver rocket with ominous unintelligible words in a deep, booming, truly terrifying voice. Listening to it from behind the front door, Emily felt a prickling sensation at the back of her neck.

Emily was the last defence. If any bold adolescent had the resilience to ring the doorbell, she would open the door very slowly, shining an unseen torch to illuminate her fangs, and say softly, 'Come in!' And as she smiled, a sharp side tooth would pierce the capsule hidden in her mouth, and fake blood would run over her lips and down her chin. In fact she only once had to go this far, facing a plump pale boy of at least fourteen, who was carrying far more sweets than he deserved in a pillowcase. He squeaked at the sight of the blood and backed away, bug-eyed, keeping just enough presence of mind to clutch his pillowcase away from the reaching hands of the Ice Death and the Fire Burst.

The Boggart paused briefly in his invisible activities and looked down at the Gang with approving surprise. He had never seen such subtle and lifelike tricks used by ordinary humans before, in the annual struggle to keep the Cailleach Bheur at bay. They were almost worthy of a boggart.

But then he forgot them instantly, and his eyes widened, as he saw approaching in the shadows, dim-lit and terrible, the dark hunched figure of the winter hag herself. There she was, tapping with her stick at trees and bushes, advancing on him. Her blue face glowed pale and ghastly; she drew closer and closer, and he could feel already the icy breath that would clamp the long dead months of winter over the lochs and hills like a shroud. She was on her way to eat up this house, to envelop it in ice. But he was ready for her! They were fortunate, this foolish unprepared family, that they had a boggart to take precautions for them! He dived hastily back towards the house.

And as the stooped figure of the Cailleach Bheur turned in from the dark street, all hell broke loose. A chair hurtled from one bedroom window, smashing into pieces on the ground; a bookcase from another, scattering books that did not drop as they should, but seemed to drift down through the air, their pages fluttering like the wings of birds. There was a loud shrieking voice, calling out words in a language nobody could understand, and from both sides of the house great blasts of icy water leaped forward at the blue-faced hag, and she crumpled into a heap of dark clothes on the ground.

The water fell away, and the voice dropped into silence. In the darkness the children moved again, out of a sudden appalled paralysis. Emily came down the path from the front door. She bent down by the figure in the dark witch robe, and pulled off the blue plastic mask that was held over the face by a rubber band.

It was Maggie, blinking up at her in reproach and the beginnings of rage.

CHAPTER EIGHT

MAGGIE VOLNIK was an awesome sight when very angry, even wearing a dressing gown, with her hair wrapped in a towel. She seemed to be even angrier now than she had been a few moments ago, when she stalked inside to pull off her wet clothes. She stood on the stairs, glaring down at them.

'I go to the trouble of dressing up to surprise you, because you aren't allowed out, and what happens? You half drown me! You smash the furniture! And on top of everything else you have to destroy Bob's beloved holly bush! What's the matter with you kids? Have you completely lost your minds?'

Emily said blankly, 'The holly bush?'

'Oh, for Pete's sake, Emily, who are you kidding?

There are holly branches all over the house – every window, every mantelpiece –' Maggie's voice was quivering with rage. 'What the hell were you doing, playing Christmas? And that insane booby trap – you could have killed me! I thought you were responsible people, not half-witted two-year-olds!'

In a silent group they gaped up at her, baffled and shaken, all feeling suddenly ridiculous in their Halloween gear. Jessup gave a loud sniff. Barry shifted uneasily, his legs and lower body still encased in the bottom half of the rocket. He said in a low voice, 'Mrs Volnik, I swear, no one had any –'

'And you!' Maggie yelled at him, jabbing a finger through the air. 'What do you think you're doing, playing with ten-year-olds at your age? You're sick! Did you dream up this nasty little enterprise, eh? Is this your coked-up idea of being funny?'

'*Stop it!*' Emily shrieked. Her voice was so loud it startled her as much as everyone else. But now she in turn was angry with Maggie, and she wasn't stopping to think. 'Barry didn't do a thing, none of us did a thing! You always blame people without knowing what you're talking about! How could we throw furniture out of the windows if we were all right down there on the street? It wasn't us!'

'Then who was it?' Maggie snapped. 'Burglars?'

Emily took a deep breath. Several black velvet ribbons from her wig fell across her eyes, and she pulled the wig off impatiently. 'Maybe . . . maybe the house is haunted.'

'Ha!' It was half a scornful laugh, half a sneer. Maggie pulled a handful of the same black ribbons from her pocket, and held them up. 'Pretty smart ghost, to use your ribbons to tie holly branches over my windows.'

In his pyjamas, Jessup tiptoed across the landing to Emily's door. A floorboard creaked, and he paused, but there was no movement downstairs. He could hear a faint murmur of voices from the sitting room. Robert had come home late and was now no doubt hearing an outraged recital from Maggie.

Jessup opened the door, very carefully. 'Em?' he whispered.

Emily switched on the angle lamp beside her bed, and tilted it down so that it gave only a little light. Even so, he could see that she had been crying.

'Shut the door,' she whispered back.

Jessup turned the knob, silently, and came and

sat on the edge of her bed. He said softly, 'In case you wondered, it wasn't me either.'

'I know,' Emily said. 'It wasn't anybody. Not anybody real.'

Jessup wrinkled his nose, in the way he did in his maths class, when the teacher offered an answer that Jessup knew was inaccurate.

'Listen,' said Emily. 'I know you're a genius, I know you understand lots of things I don't, I know you only believe in facts and figures. But you've seen all this impossible stuff happening, right?'

'Right,' said Jessup. He looked unhappily at her swollen eyes. 'Are you OK, Em?'

'I'm fine,' Emily said. She gave him a faint, grateful smile. 'Listen,' she said again. 'I was talking about it at the theatre, to Dai Rees and Willie Walker.'

'Ah,' said Jessup with respect. Everyone connected with the Chervil company had a vague but powerful sense that there was something special about Dai and Willie, their two native-born Celts.

'They were different from anyone else,' Emily said. 'They believed straight away that we had nothing to do with all this stuff. And they knew about it, they said it comes from a . . . from a sort of invisible creature, that likes playing tricks. Not a ghost. But not human.'

'Not . . . human?'

'No.'

Jessup said hopefully, 'An alien?'

'No. From Scotland and Wales and old places like that. Very old. Magic.'

'Magic,' Jessup said slowly, as if he were tasting the word.

'It likes to live with a family, and play jokes, Dai and Willie said. They said it might have come with us from Scotland. It's called a boggart.'

There was a brief, faint rustling sound from Emily's bookshelf. Jessup glanced into the shadows. 'What's that?'

'I dunno. A mouse. Jess, we have to go talk to Willie.'

'Yeah,' Jessup said.

The Boggart was dancing on the edge of the bookshelf, delighted. He had been lying in a resentful half sleep, but when Emily had spoken his name he had shot up into the air, wide awake, filled with joy. They had recognized him! Finally, after all this time in this very strange place, they had realized that he was there! For the first time since the MacDevon had died, he could begin living with friends!

Emily was explaining to Jessup, in as much detail as she could remember, everything that

Willie and Dai had said about boggarts. 'The amazing part was the way they recognized everything I was describing. Willie just said straight away, *It's a boggart.* Like you turn on a tap, and someone says, *That's water.*'

'There's a lot of questions to ask,' Jessup said. He stood up – then paused suddenly, looking surprised. He touched his cheek.

'What's the matter?' said Emily – and then paused, and put her hand up to her own face. She looked at Jessup with a strange expression that was a mixture of astonishment and total disbelief.

Jessup said, bemused, 'It was like someone stroked my cheek. Someone's hand.'

'That's right,' Emily said. 'A very small hand.'

They stared at each other.

Somewhere in the room, faint, growing, there was a slow happy sound like the purring of a cat.

'Is Polly in here?' said Jessup.

Emily said shakily, 'No.'

Aunt Jen said brightly, 'Well, I'm glad to see you, whatever the circumstances. And it's always nice to have help on Dusting Day.'

Emily said resentfully, 'Mom only had to ask us to help – she knew we'd have come. But she has to turn it into this great huge punishment deal. *You will spend Saturday working at the shop!* As if we hadn't been helping at the shop ever since we were little!'

Aunt Jen gave her a comforting hug, and produced a handful of dusting cloths from the pocket of her voluminous jumper. Dusting Day came once a week at Old Stuff. It was a tedious process from which not only every piece of furniture but every small object, from roasting pan to thimble, had to emerge dust free and sparkling to attract the customers.

'Silver cloth for Em, standard for Jess,' she said, handing out the dusters. 'And for Pete's sake don't break anything.'

'Are you kidding?' said Jessup with feeling. 'She'd *atomize* us!'

'You've all been having a difficult time,' said Aunt Jen diplomatically. She was always careful not to take sides in Volnik family tussles. 'Do a great job, and things'll get better. Maggie will be back soon – she's picking something up from Customs.'

She disappeared into the back of the shop, and Emily and Jessup began their dusting, very carefully indeed. Jessup took six champagne glasses off a shelf, polished the shelf and each glass, and put the last glass back with a sigh of relief. Emily polished a silver coffee pot, cream jug and sugar bowl. 'Good thing that boggart's not here,' she said.

'Why holly?' Jessup said.

'What?'

'He put holly branches over all the windows. He must have had a reason.'

'I don't think it has real reasons for anything,' said Emily wearily. 'It just likes bothering people. I mean what reason would it have for putting a squishy sandwich on your chair, except playing a silly joke?'

'I don't think he's an *it* –' Jessup began, but the door of the shop opened and their mother came in, carrying a cardboard carton. Emily looked up warily, and saw behind Maggie a tall, dark, grave man whom she felt she had seen before, though she couldn't remember when or where.

'Emily, Jessup,' said Maggie, formal and brisk. 'This is Dr Stigmore.'

'Good morning,' said the man.

'Hi,' said Jessup.

'Hello,' said Emily. She started to polish a box full of silver-plated knives and forks, all set neatly in rows.

Sitting on the open lid of the box, the Boggart looked across at Maggie, resentfully. He had come to the shop, clinging invisibly and uncomfortably to the handlebars of Emily's bicycle, because he wanted to be with his two new friends – not with this woman who had dared to dress up as the Cailleach Bheur. Someone had described her costume that night as the Wicked Witch of the West, whatever that might be, but he knew better. The Boggart felt disappointed. He was not good at coping with more than one emotion at once, and the sight of Maggie had brought a shadow over his newly discovered happiness. He made a small self-pitying sound, and it vibrated through the air of the shop like the whimper of a lost puppy.

Emily and Jessup stiffened, and looked nervously at each other.

'What did you say?' Maggie said, pausing.

'Nothing,' said Emily.

'Nothing,' said Jessup.

'We're just dusting,' Emily said. 'Very carefully.'

'Good,' said her mother. She gave them a last suspicious glance and beckoned the dark man into the room at the rear of the shop. 'It's in here, Dr Stigmore. The largest piece we brought back ... too large for you perhaps, but it would go well with your desk ...'

They disappeared. Jessup said, 'It's the creep.'

'So it is,' Emily said. That was why he had looked familiar: he was the bad-tempered man who had bought her roll-top desk. Well, now she had one of her own, so there, and it was nicer than his and had come all the way from the castle.

Emily paused suddenly. Through her mind there floated an image of Ron and Jim the delivery men, struggling to bring the little Scottish desk up the stairs to her room. It had lurched erratically all over the place, and in the end seemed to tip itself on to Jim's foot. *'It's bewitched!'* Ron had said . . .

She looked uncertainly around the shop. 'I don't think that noise was anything, do you?' she said to Jessup.

'Course not!' said Jessup heartily, hoping he was right.

The Boggart watched with approval as Emily and Jessup dusted and polished. He felt relaxed again now that the three of them were alone. *My friends!* he thought joyously. He was filled with the instinct for happy meaningless mischief which was his normal state of mind, and debated with himself how best to share it with them. What could he do that would make them smile?

Emily finished polishing the silverware, closed the box and reached up to put it back on its shelf.

Then she glanced across the shop and stood frozen, staring.

A small rag doll was climbing out of a box of antique toys which stood on a table at the far end of the shop. Another followed it, and then a third. The third had its head missing, but seemed not to mind. The three dolls stood on the table facing Emily, holding hands in a line, and they began to dance, floppily, first in one direction and then back again. One-two-three, hop, one-two-three, hop, one-two-three, hop –

'Uurgh!' said Emily, in a strangled, stricken voice, and Jessup looked up swiftly. His eyes widened, and he dropped the glass he was polishing – and instead of falling to the ground the glass floated back to the shelf from which it had come. The dolls danced on, one-two-three, hop, one-two-three, hop, and not far away an antique dressmaker's dummy began to sway to the same rhythm. So did the silk flowers in a vase on the other side of the shop, and the tall dried grasses standing in an empty World War II shell case. So did the group of chandeliers hanging from the ceiling, making a gentle jingling, tinkling sound. On the face of every clock in the shop – and there were more than a dozen – the hands began twirling gaily around and

around. Very gently, the shop began to vibrate to the beat of the dolls' slow dance, and Emily and Jessup looked at each other, and began to smile.

'He's doing it for us!' Jessup said, entranced. 'He's putting on a show!'

Emily called out softly, into the air, 'It's lovely, Boggart!'

An umbrella stand full of umbrellas gave a small drunken lurch, and one by one the umbrellas flew up out of it to the ceiling, and opened, and hung there like bright hovering parachutes, swaying in time. A handsome brocade armchair rose three feet off the ground, slow and stately, and so did an old wooden church pew, creaking. One-two-three, hop, one-two-three, hop . . . Like a final flourish, a round table covered with a set of twelve delicate crystal glasses rose up, and up, and hovered, and Emily laughed in delight, but quivered in terror lest it too began swaying to the rhythm of the dance.

She called out, laughing, '*Careful –*'

And Maggie came back into the shop from the room at the back, followed by Dr Stigmore, and the table and glasses dropped to the ground with a terrible crash. Maggie screamed.

Dolls, clocks, chandeliers were instantly still,

but there was a whirling like a trapped flock of birds as the umbrellas folded back into their stand. The armchair lurched to the floor, Dr Stigmore pulled Maggie out of the way as the heavy church pew floated through the air and down.

There was a moment of dreadful breathless silence, and Emily panicked. There had been so many accusations – now there would be more. She couldn't bear it. She shrieked, 'It wasn't us! It wasn't us!' – and she seized Jessup by the arm and ran with him out of the door, out into the street and away.

Dr Stigmore had Maggie sitting in one of the antique armchairs with her head down between her knees; he was patting her on the back and murmuring gently. Aunt Jen stood by, anxious, baffled; she had come running after Maggie's scream, and seen nothing but the upturned table in a small sea of broken glass. Emily and Jessup were gone, and her partner was sobbing hysterically. She looked helplessly at Dr Stigmore.

He was glowing. She had never seen him smile before. 'Amazing!' he said. 'Quite amazing! An absolutely classic poltergeist manifestation! I've never seen anything like it! This is really one for the record books!'

'What happened?' said Aunt Jen, her round face pale and troubled. She bent over Maggie, stroking her neck.

Maggie tried to pull herself together; she sat up, sniffing. 'It was terrible – it was like last night! Furniture flying through the air, things crashing around as if the place was possessed! Oh, Jen – it was terrifying!' Her voice began to quiver again.

'Now don't worry,' said Dr Stigmore soothingly. 'This can all be explained. No possession here, no demons and exorcists, dear me no!' He paused, looking keenly at Maggie. 'What do you mean, *like last night*?'

'It happened at home too,' Maggie said wretchedly. 'Funny things have been happening for a while, but this was the worst – a chair and a bookcase flying out the window – water spraying; I thought it was the children, but now I see it couldn't have been.' She clung to Aunt Jen's hand.

'There, there,' said Aunt Jen, totally baffled.

Dr Stigmore pushed back his thick dark hair, his face bright with professional enthusiasm. 'Well, in a way it probably is the children, or one of them. Poltergeist phenomena are classically linked with the emotions of a disturbed adolescent. His or her rage produces the psychokinesis – you see!' He beamed at them.

'The what?' said Aunt Jen.

Maggie said rebelliously, 'My kids aren't disturbed! They aren't even adolescent! Oh dear –' Her face crumpled again.

'There, there, honey,' said Aunt Jen.

'Psychokinesis is a force by which the power of the mind is said to move physical objects,' Dr Stigmore said.

'Oh dear,' said Aunt Jen.

CHAPTER NINE

THE THEATRE was full of the scurry and
bustle of technical rehearsals, and one of the
busiest places of all, backstage, was the wardrobe
room. Emily and Jessup sidled in, trying to look
as inconspicuous as possible. Dai had his mouth
full of pins, and was busy shortening the tunic of
an actor who stood on a chair with his eyes closed,
silently reciting lines. Two wardrobe assistants
were hunched over sewing machines, and a third
was fitting tall boots on to a life-size dummy with
no head, which lay spreadeagled across a table.
For an instant Emily thought of the Boggart's
dancing dolls. Then Dai caught sight of her.

'Mmmf,' he said through the pins, managing

to sound welcoming, concerned and apologetic all at once.

'Can we do anything useful?' Emily said timidly.

'Yes!' said the assistant with the boots. 'Hold this bloody dummy while I give him his feet.'

Emily and Jessup shoved at the dummy's headless shoulders while the assistant shoved the boots at the other end. 'Who is he?' Jessup said.

'He's me, after I get knocked off,' said the actor, and looking at him, they realized that his costume was identical to the dummy's. Dai finished pinning his tunic, and patted his leg dismissively. The actor jumped off the chair and made Emily and Jessup a sweeping bow. 'Cloten, at your service,' he said.

'Act Four beginners, Act Four beginners,' said a metallic voice from a speaker on the wall.

'Whoops!' said Cloten, and he grabbed a sword belt and scurried out of the door, buckling it on. Two of the assistants scrambled after him with the dummy.

Dai looked hard at Emily and Jessup. 'What's up?' he said.

Emily tried to sound casual. 'Is Willie around?'

'It's that boggart, isn't it?' said Dai.

'It sure is,' Jessup said.

'He'll be in, but only for a minute. This is the first tech run-through – your father and Phil are setting light cues.'

Phil was Philip Warrior, the lighting designer for *Cymbeline*. Emily said helpfully to Jessup, 'They watch the play and decide how the lighting has to change, all the way through.'

'I *know*,' said Jessup irritably. The computerized board from which the lights were controlled was the only thing in the Chervil Playhouse that really interested him.

Their father's voice yelled faintly from the loudspeaker, 'Joe! The mike on this board is on the fritz!'

'Oh dear,' said Dai. 'Trouble.'

Willie came hurrying in, with a young actress who was one of Emily's favourite people in the company. Her name was Meg Bootle; she was a quiet girl with long blonde hair. Offstage few people noticed her; onstage her voice was strong and musical and she was suddenly beautiful. Although Emily knew her own destiny was to save the whales, she often wished she had been born with the talents of Meg Bootle. Just for once, though, she wished Meg were somewhere else; she desperately wanted Willie's advice about the Boggart.

Meg was dressed as a young man, in vaguely Elizabethan tights and tunic. Willie looked extremely strange in a costume made of strips of leather and fur, with long boots and a very peculiar feathered bonnet. He whipped this last from his head and dropped it fastidiously on the floor.

'Robert killed the hat, thank God. And he says the boots are too high.'

Dai said cautiously, 'What did Sarah say?' Sarah was the costume designer.

'She said, *Have Dai fix them*.'

'All right then.' Dai dropped on his knees beside Willie and began folding down the boot tops.

Jessup said, 'Who are you playing, Willie?'

'Hello, my loves!' Willie turned to beam at them. He struck a heroic attitude. 'I am Belarius, a lord from the court of Cymbeline, disguised as a rural hick. Twenty years ago he banished me, so I pinched his two baby sons and have disguised *them* as rural hicks ever since. Imogen here –' he took Meg's hand – 'is Cymbeline's daughter, disguised as a young man, who is being chased by her evil stepbrother disguised as her husband. Don't you wish you hadn't asked that question?'

'It gets worse,' said Meg cheerfully. 'Where are the safety pins, Dai?'

'Em knows,' Dai said, busy with Willie's left boot. Emily hastened to fetch the safety-pin box, but just as she reached for it, it jumped to the shelf below. *Oh no!* thought Emily. She reached again, swiftly, but the box jumped sideways to a table – where she managed to grab it with her other hand, just in time. She heard a faint ripple of sound in the air, like an echo of laughter.

Meg hadn't noticed. 'Thank you, darling,' she said, and busied herself with the pins. But Willie was looking hard at Emily.

He said gently, 'Has someone been giving you problems, Em?'

Emily nodded unhappily. 'I don't know what to do,' she said. 'And now he's followed us here too.'

'Hold on,' said Willie. 'We'll think of something.'

The loudspeaker crackled, and Robert's faint voice said, 'OK, let's go! Act Four!'

Willie turned to go. 'You going to watch this rigmarole?' he said. 'Sit at the back, and I'll get to you when I can; through Robert's door.'

Robert's door was in the back wall of the auditorium, next to the window behind which the stage manager sat working the light board. It was a very small and discreet door, and had been especially cut a few years before so that Robert could slip in and out of a back-row seat during performances without being seen by what he described as 'the dreaded audience'. It opened on to a walkway next to the little room which enclosed the light board, and a staircase ran down from it and led, eventually, to the area backstage. The whole theatre was like a small rabbit warren, which Emily knew very well and Jessup hardly at all.

Emily led her brother up the staircase to the door, opened it very quietly and let him in. Before following, she half closed the door again and turned to face the stairwell. She said to the empty air, in a whisper, 'Boggart, *please* don't do anything to get us into trouble here.'

There was silence. Emily tried to sense whether anyone invisible was there, and failed. She sighed, and went into the auditorium, and the Boggart flittered in with her. He felt wounded by the implication that he might ever intend to damage anyone. Didn't the girl know that boggarts live for mischief, not for harm?

Jessup and Emily sat quietly in the back row, hoping nobody would notice them. Robert was halfway down the auditorium, sitting with two other people at a table which had been laid across the tops of several seats. They wore earphones, and had microphones and muted lights on the table in front of them.

The stage had been made into a rocky landscape, with real trees and bushes, and in front of the bushes stood Cloten, looking around him belligerently. '*Posthumus,*' he was saying, '*thy head, which now is growing on thy shoulders, shall within this hour be off!*' It was not clear whom he was talking to, because he was alone on the stage, but he grew very fierce and drew his sword. As he spoke, down in the stalls the lighting designer muttered into his microphone, and the light on the stage grew brighter and then darker again, and then very bright, as if it were first afternoon, then evening, then early morning. Cloten marched off the stage, waving his sword, and two of the bushes moved gracefully sideways, to reveal the entrance to a cave. There was a yell from the group huddled around Robert in the stalls. 'Hold it!'

The Boggart watched all this in speechless delight. From the moment he entered the auditorium, he had been enchanted. This building held a small world in which he felt instantly totally at home; a world of magic, where the rules of ordinary human life seemed not to apply. A wooden floor could become a living forest; an actor with pins stuck all around his tunic could become a wild young man threatening murder; night could become day. The Boggart was particularly entranced by the lighting changes. That was more than he could manage in his world. How did they do it? He flittered down over the seats to Robert's table, inquisitive.

Robert was studying the stage. 'Too warm, don't you think?' he said to one of the men with earphones.

'Let's pull down the amber on the cyc,' said the man into his microphone. 'Ten points, OK?'

The Boggart did not find this helpful. He flittered on around the theatre, up on to the stage, where he looked up and saw the battery of light instruments hanging from the roof grid, blazing at him; out again into the darkness of the auditorium. At the back of the house he saw a square of light and flittered over to investigate that. Behind the window he saw the stage manager sitting at the light board, wearing earphones, her fingers playing with a keyboard as the Boggart had seen Jessup play with his computer. The computer had never seemed of much interest to the Boggart, but this keyboard, it appeared, was the source of every change in that magical array of lights over the stage. Fascinated, the Boggart began looking for a way into the little room.

Under the light board, docile old Fred the theatre dog lifted his head from the stage manager's feet, his ears suddenly erect. He jumped to his feet, nearly knocking the stage manager out of her chair, and began barking hysterically.

'Shut up, Fred!' said the stage manager irritably.

Fred barked louder. He bared his teeth, snarling between barks, straining to see out of the window into the theatre. The stage manager whacked at him ineffectually, trying to hear the instructions squawking into her headset. Fred swung around and began barking at the door, leaping up at it, whining, frantic.

'Get out, then, you idiot!' yelled the stage manager, and she pulled the door open. Fred tumbled out in a clamour of barks and yelps – and just before the door closed, the Boggart flittered calmly in.

Fred sniffed the air, snarled and reversed himself, attacking the door again in a noisy frenzy. A passing stagehand seized him by the collar and dragged him away.

The play went on. Onstage, out of the entrance to the cave came Willie, booming away in his leathery costume, with Meg dressed as a young man, and two real young men dressed in the same curious fashion as Willie. Emily and Jessup sat watching in the back row. The two young men seemed to be brothers, and to think that Meg was also their brother. They were going hunting, but when they weren't looking Meg secretly and mysteriously swallowed some kind of drug, and retreated into the cave to sleep. Then Cloten came on with his sword, and was left alone with one of the young men, Polydore, whom he rudely called a 'villain mountaineer'. They began to fight.

Jessup loved the fight, and tried not to bounce in his seat. Cloten had a sword and Polydore had only a dagger, but was clearly going to win. It was at the end of the fight, as they clashed their way offstage, that the lights in the theatre began to go mad.

The changes were gradual, but extraordinary. At first, the brightness of the lighting remained the same, but it took on a faint reddish tinge, growing stronger in colour until it was a deep scarlet. From the cries of consternation in Robert's group, Emily realized this was not a light cue planned by the director or his designer. She crept out of her seat and down the aisle until she was in earshot, and heard her father uttering a number of four-letter words he did not normally use in her presence. In the darkness, she grinned to herself.

The lighting began to change colour again, and she realized that it was going very slowly through the spectrum: red, orange, yellow . . . Jessup slipped into a seat beside her. On the stage, the actors, occasionally looking nervously up at the light grid, went on speaking their lines, probably because Robert was too busy cursing to tell them to stop. As the lights began to turn from yellow to green, Polydore came back on stage proudly holding Cloten's chopped-off head aloft. Emily heard Jessup cheer beside her.

The lights began to darken to blue. The lighting designer was shouting into his microphone. Up in the light booth the stage manager was waving her arms about. Onstage, just as the lights changed from blue to indigo and began to merge into purple, Willie came deliberately down to the front of the stage and recited his next lines straight at Robert.

He boomed:
'O *thou goddess,*
Thou divine nature, thou thyself thou blazon'st
In these two princely boys! They are as gentle
As zephyrs blowing below the violet –'

Willie paused. 'Vi-o-let!' he said pointedly. 'Who's running the light board – Shakespeare?'

Emily said softly, 'No – the Boggart.'

'Oh my gosh!' said Jessup in horror.

Ahead of them Robert called back grimly. 'Just keep going, Willie.'

'Never trust a computer,' said Willie. He went back to his Shakespeare voice. '*They are as gentle . . .*'

Jessup craned his head to look back at the window behind which the stage manager and an electrician were both now flapping their arms. He hissed at Emily, 'You really think he's in there operating the board, invisible?'

'Either that or he's inside it,' Emily said.

'*Inside it?*'

But then the lights made a different kind of change. The purple glow which dominated the stage faded swiftly away into a clear light like early morning, fresh and cool. It seemed to ripple gently, as if wisps of cloud were floating over an unseen sun.

'Now that's more like it!' said Robert in relief. 'What gobo is that, Phil?'

'I'm not sure,' said the designer. He peered at the stage nervously.

'It's beautiful!' Robert said. He settled back

happily into his seat, and on the stage the actors' voices began to lose the tension that had made them all, even Willie, sound much higher-pitched than normal. Polydore came back onstage and announced that he had sent Cloten's chopped-off head floating down the stream, and as Willie laughed the light seemed to laugh with him, taking on a wonderfully brilliant gaiety. Then unexpected the theatre filled with deep, slow, solemn music, and the actors expressed surprise and the light seemed to glimmer with it too.

'Lovely!' said Robert, enchanted. 'I don't know what you're doing, but it's perfect!'

The lighting designer made a small strangled noise of baffled gratitude, and whispered frantically into his microphone.

On this stage, Polydore's brother entered, carrying Meg in his arms. He didn't know she was only asleep after taking the mysterious drug – he thought she was dead, and so did Polydore and Willie. Watching the way Meg let her body droop into emptiness, so did Emily. 'O *melancholy!*' cried Willie, and the light filling the stage became muted and strange, like an embodiment of grief.

'Oh yes!' cried Robert in delight. He clapped Phil the lighting designer on the back.

'What is that?' hissed Phil into his microphone to the stage manager at the light board.

But the stage manager didn't know. Watching, admiring but desperate, she knew she would never be able to reproduce the wonderful effects the computer was instructing the lights to shine at the stage – because she was not controlling the computer. It was taking no notice of any instructions she punched into its keyboard. It was designing the lighting pattern itself.

And inside the computer, the Boggart was beside himself with delight. He had taken the lights through the spectrum of all the colours as an exercise, a way of teaching himself how to use them. Now, he knew the language of light and he was speaking it. By his own magic, he was using the magic of this new technological world in which he found himself – and the mixing of the two magics was a wonder. In the theatre, Emily and Jessup and all the company members watched it without daring to breathe, knowing they had never seen anything like this on a stage before. Lyrical and mysterious, the lights shifted and flickered and glowed, like echoes of the words the bemused actors were saying on the stage.

They lasted until the song. It was a song of

mourning over the supposed dead body of Meg/
Imogen, and its words were not actually sung, but
spoken, because the character Polydore in the play
claimed that he would weep if he tried to sing.
('Shakespeare wrote it that way because he had an
actor with a lousy singing voice,' Robert told them
pithily, much later.) But the words themselves, having
been written by the man who was the greatest master
of the English language who will ever live, held an
enchantment that cut right through the Boggart's
magic to the Boggart himself. They reached his
heart, and found in it the old deep sorrow of his
double loss: the deaths of the only two human
beings he had loved, Duncan and Devon MacDevon.

> *Fear no more the heat o' the sun*
> *Nor the furious winter's rages;*
> *Thou thy worldly task hast done,*
> *Home art gone, and ta'en thy wages.*
> *Golden lads and girls all must,*
> *As chimney-sweepers, come to dust . . .*

The words overwhelmed the Boggart, filling
him with a terrible grief at the loss not only of
Duncan and the MacDevon, but of his own home.
He came blundering out of the computer that

governed the theatre lights, and flittered back unthinking into the auditorium. He was filled with love and grief and longing, and the force of his feeling took hold of everyone inside the theatre, on the stage or behind it or in front of it.

The whole place was possessed by his sorrowing. Like a dark cloud it swallowed the consciousness of everyone listening. Emily felt a misery blacker than anything she had ever felt before; Jessup felt himself a desolate deserted baby, wanting to howl for his mother; Robert was back in the bleakest moment of his own much longer life, the moment he tried always unsuccessfully to forget, and so was every grown man or woman there.

The voices of the two actors went on, clear, intertwining.

> *No exorciser harm thee!*
> *Nor no witchcraft charm thee!*
> *Ghost unlaid forbear thee!*
> *Nothing ill come near thee!*
> *Quiet consummation have,*
> *And renowned be thy grave!*

The voices fell silent. And in the dim light that was left, gradually the theatre began to fill with an eerie sound which belonged not to the play but to the Boggart, to the pain of life and loss that he was feeling. Soft, faraway, coming closer, there was the throb of a muffled drumbeat, *ta-rum* . . . *ta-rum* . . . *ta-rum* . . . and over it the plaintive music of a lament played on a single bagpipe; and over that too, like an echo, the curious husky sound of the shuffling of many feet.

The sound grew and grew, louder and louder, closer and closer, intolerably close and loud, filling the theatre so that all the listeners inside it longed to flatten their hands against their ears to shut out the terrible wave of grief. Then at the peak of the noise it was gone, vanished, and the light died with it, leaving the theatre silent and dark.

CHAPTER TEN

A GLIMMER OF light came into the back of the dark theatre, as someone opened the little hidden door near the light booth. Emily turned to look. In the bright oblong she saw the outline of Willie's figure, and heard him say softly, 'Emily? Jessup?'

They shook themselves out of the spell of emotion, and scurried up the aisle towards him. As they went out, Robert's voice came sharply after them. 'Emily? Is that you?'

Emily shut the voice behind the door, and ran down the stairs with Jessup and Willie following. Nobody came after them. *Too many other problems*, Emily thought. She pushed open the outside door and paused in the tree-lined street. A flurry of falling leaves whirled around her head.

Just before Willie let the door swing back behind them, the Boggart came flittering out and settled, unseen, unheard, on Jessup's shoulder.

Willie took a deep breath, and shook his head as if to get rid of what was inside it. 'Poor unhappy creature!' he said. 'What a terrible sadness!'

Relief flooded through Emily's head. 'You mean that was him too? I knew the lights were, but I was afraid –'

'You were afraid it was in your own mind, I dare say,' said Willie, looking at her keenly. 'Well, it was not.' He was a strange figure, with his costume hidden under an overcoat but his grey hair wild and flowing, and his eyes darkly outlined with make-up in an orange-brown face. He glanced back reluctantly at the theatre 'I can't leave, but you must go home, straight home. He'll go with you – he's a family fellow. Call me tonight – I'll try to work out what to do. This mannie is so strong, and so far out of his element, there's no knowing what he may get up to if he's not checked.'

Jessup said nervously, 'He gets up to things at home too.'

'But smaller things,' Willie said. 'That's the

scale he's used to, that's where he belongs. He surely doesn't belong in a theatre light board.'

'Wasn't that marvellous?' Emily was filled with wonder again as she remembered the magical shifting lights on the stage.

'Remember it,' Willie said. 'You'll never see the like again.' He patted her shoulder, ruffled Jessup's hair and went back into the theatre.

The Boggart had not listened to a word they said, and he had only a vague dwindling memory of the ferocious grief which had poured out of him minutes before. The weather changed very fast, in his odd boggart heart. He was busy watching a pair of city pigeons in the gutter, and wondering how best to creep up on them and tweak their tail feathers. The trickster was back at doing what he did best, and with most pleasure: inventing tricks.

'Come on,' Emily said to Jessup. She set off very fast down the street, and around the corner into the streets where the houses were, with their cherished small front gardens. They passed one still bright with tawny chrysanthemums; another neatly arrayed with late vegetables, set out in decorative precision as if they were flowers. The Boggart flittered down and stole a Brussels sprout, then went back to Jessup's shoulder and sat there nibbling it, raw. He had not seen very much of Toronto, but his favourite parts were those where people clearly had homes, rather than enormous piles of concrete like inferior copies of cliffs.

Emily and Jessup turned another corner. 'You think Mom will be back?' Jessup said.

'Oh glory,' Emily said. She walked more slowly, as her head filled with all the images of flying furniture in her mother's shop. 'What are we going to tell her?'

'It's more what she'll tell *us*,' Jessup said.

Emily said despondently, 'They'll never believe us, either of them.'

'Well, Dad saw those light effects. And felt that . . . that whatever it was. The sadness.'

'They'll have some really sensible explanation,' Emily said wearily. She stopped in the middle of the pavement, and looked around her. 'Where are you, Boggart?' she demanded.

The Boggart, hearing his name, looked at her thoughtfully from Jessup's shoulder. These children were singularly poorly educated, compared to children of an earlier age. Had nobody ever told them that boggarts do not speak to human beings?

Emily said, 'If we could just talk to him!'

'He likes food,' Jessup said suddenly.

'What?'

'The peanut-butter sandwich, the jar of fudge sauce – the sausage Dad said I took off his plate last Sunday morning. Those were all him, I bet you. He's greedy. I think we should go into Bund's and buy him some ice cream.'

The Boggart beamed, and licked his lips.

Emily hesitated, then nodded. 'OK. It's worth trying.' She searched her pockets, and found some crumpled dollar bills. 'All right, Boggart,' she said to the air. 'Now you get to choose whether you want butter pecan or black raspberry. But you'll have to *tell us*.'

They ran down the road and around another corner, the Boggart clinging to Jessup's collar, and in a little while they came to a major thoroughfare. The Boggart flinched, and clung tighter. It was the first main road he had seen, close up, and he was amazed by the roaring traffic, the crowds of people, the noise and the flashing lights. He stared at the neon sign glowing over the window of the ice-cream shop as they went in; he gazed down in greedy astonishment at the tubs of eighteen different flavours of ice cream. And before anyone could ask him, silently and invisibly he sent the hand and scoop of the girl behind the counter to the tub of his favourite, vanilla ice cream.

Emily saw the girl looking uncertainly at her own hand as it served out the ice cream, and she said swiftly, 'And one mint chocolate chip and one coffee.'

'You did say vanilla?' the girl said, dazed.

'Sure,' Emily said kindly and untruthfully. She was beginning to feel that as a ruse for making the Boggart show himself, this was not going to work.

They took their three dishes of ice cream to a table like a tall mushroom, at which they stood. Bund's was a shop with many customers and not much space. 'There you go, Boggart,' Emily said, and she put the vanilla ice cream in the middle of the table. She and Jessup watched it closely as they spooned up their own, but nothing happened. Instead, the neon sign in the window reading BUND'S ICE CREAM began to flash, off and on, off and on, in time to the rock music which filled the air. Like everyone else in the shop, Emily and Jessup stared at it. There was no way of telling whether the flashing was accidental or deliberate, though it was undoubtedly happening to the same beat as the music.

When Emily looked back at the table, the dish

of vanilla ice cream was empty. She thought she saw the very last mouthful disappear, as if it had evaporated.

Jessup was looking too. He said belligerently to the invisible Boggart, 'Well, was it good?'

'Delicious, thank you,' said an old lady standing at the next table, a spoonful of strawberry ice cream about to disappear into her mouth. She smiled at him. 'How sweet of you to ask!'

Jessup tried to spread a sickly insincere grin over his face, but he never had to finish it, because at that point the lights went out. Then they came back, then flickered out again. The neon sign in the shop window was still flashing to the music. And beyond it, outside, suddenly the darkening street seemed to be filled with blue fire. They heard muffled shouts and screams.

'What's he doing?' Jessup said, appalled. He glimpsed the dismay on Emily's face, and then they were both diving for the door.

From his perch on the table, the Boggart had noticed the tram wires over the street. Realizing that they must carry the same magical power that seemed to make everything work in this city, he saw an irresistible chance to play tricks on all the people in those trams. Out he went, joyously, and flittered up to a wire junction, and he began playing with the power in the wires just as he had played with the channels in the Volniks' television set. He cut off the power from one tram just as it reached the centre of an intersection; sent another one humming down the street even though the startled driver was trying to stop; dived back to the first to give it power again just as the second tram seemed about to crash into it. An old man at the back of the first tram fainted. People watching in the streets screamed. Electricity danced along the wires like blue lightning.

The Boggart laughed like a delighted small child, and looked around for another kind of game. The traffic lights caught his eye.

Below him in the street, among the panicking crowds, Emily and Jessup looked wildly about them for some sign of where the Boggart might be. 'He can't be far!' Emily said, frantic. 'He always stays near you or me! Oh, Willie was right – we should have gone straight home –'

'Boggart!' Jessup yelled, spinning around, looking upwards. 'Boggart, *stop it*!'

'You stay here – I'll try the other side –' And as the pedestrian signal changed to WALK Emily darted to join a group of people crossing the road.

But the Boggart was playing with the traffic lights, and though the WALK signal had changed, the green light for traffic had turned not to red but to a delicate turquoise blue. So the traffic didn't stop. There was a desperate honking of horns, a squealing of brakes; voices screamed, glass shattered, metal crashed into concrete. Jessup swung around in horror and saw that a car had crumpled its fender against a lamp post, and that two people lay unmoving in the road, and that one of them was Emily.

Emily lay looking up at the hospital ceiling, thinking about ice cream. How had the Boggart managed to eat it, without a spoon? With his hand? Did he have hands? If you couldn't feel or see or hear him, how could he be solid enough to swallow the ice cream? Not to mention all the other things he liked to eat or drink. Where did they go? Did the Boggart have to go to the loo? Did he wear clothes? Why was he a he, and not a she? Were there such things as she-boggarts? Did boggarts produce little boggarts, or did they just live forever, so that little boggarts weren't necessary?

More important than any of this, where was the Boggart now? Had he gone with Jessup, or was he lurking somewhere in this small square room, with the cream-coloured walls, the hanging television sets and the empty, neatly made second bed?

Emily sighed, tried to turn over, and remembered she couldn't. Her leg was propped up in a cast, since she had broken an ankle. Her head ached, where she had banged it on the ground; her side ached where she had somehow cracked a rib; her hip and thigh ached where, the doctor said, she was going to have a truly spectacular bruise. She had woken in the rocking ambulance, to the sound of a siren and the sight of a large efficient paramedic and a wide-eyed, damp-cheeked Jessup. Then there had been a lot of people and questions and prodding, and X-rays from assorted angles, and now here she was in the hospital for two days, though she would rather have been at home. Robert and Maggie had hovered over her with tense, worried faces, and raised no objection when the doctor murmured to them about 'keeping an eye on her, just in case'.

There was a soft knock at the door, and a tall, dark-haired man in a white coat came in, with a stethoscope dangling from his neck. Emily squinted at him over the sheet. This wasn't the doctor she had seen before.

'How are you, Emily?' he said.

Emily stiffened, in surprise and dislike. It was the creep.

'Dr Stigmore,' he said, smiling at her. She didn't trust the smile. He pulled the room's one chair from its corner and sat down beside her bed. 'Sorry to hear about your accident. How d'you feel?'

'I'm OK,' Emily said.

'I was checking a couple of my patients, so I told your mother I'd stop by. Taking good care of you, are they?'

'Fine.' She yawned, hoping he would go away. But he settled back comfortably in the chair.

'Well,' he said, 'things certainly get pretty active wherever you happen to be, don't they?'

'It was just a traffic accident,' Emily said cautiously.

'And of course you were in the street, so there weren't any chairs flying around.'

'No,' Emily said.

Dr Stigmore laughed, a little too loudly. 'I never saw anything so amazing! Lucky there wasn't more damage – that shop's full of breakable goods. I hear you've had a bunch of things like that happening at home recently too.'

'Not really,' Emily said.

'No?' He leaned forward, less casual now. 'The chair flying out the window at Halloween? And a bookcase, and books? And before that, things disappearing, and turning up in the wrong place?'

Emily tugged the bedclothes around her chin, wishing she could slide down and vanish underneath them. She said vaguely, 'Oh well . . .'

Dr Stigmore checked himself, as if he were trying not to sound too eager. He said, 'You know, Emily, growing up isn't easy, not for anyone. Maybe you've been having a tough time recently – getting angry at life. Especially at your mother. It's quite normal, you know, you don't have to feel guilty about it.'

'I don't feel guilty about anything!' said Emily, who had hardly ever exchanged a cross word with Maggie until the Boggart arrived.

He patted her blanket-wrapped shoulder. 'Of course not. None of this is your fault. It's just that all those angry feelings can produce a lot of energy, especially if you keep them hidden away. And the energy has to go somewhere, so sometimes it bursts out in ways we don't expect, and can't control. Not to worry – it won't be hard to put things right.'

Emily lay very still. She was just beginning to

realize that she was hearing an explanation for boggart behaviour invented by someone who didn't believe in boggarts.

'We'll start having some long talks when you're up on your feet again,' Dr Stigmore said. He crinkled his eyes at her reassuringly. 'Once we get rid of those feelings of yours, the trouble will go away.'

Emily gazed at him icily. 'You think *I'm* making the chairs fly about, and all that stuff?'

He went on smiling his professional smile. 'Not to worry,' he said again. 'This is a fascinating case – you're a very important person. And I assure you nobody is *blaming* you for anything.'

'I don't want any long talks,' Emily said.

'It'll be much better than feeling angry, Emily,' said Dr Stigmore. His smile began to fade; a note of irritation was creeping into his voice.

Under the bedclothes, Emily's fingers crept towards the little electric signal-button that one of the nurses had given her. *'Just press this if you need anything and we'll be right in.'* She pressed the button.

'You can't make me talk to you,' she said.

'You mustn't let yourself get angry with me too, Emily,' Dr Stigmore said. 'Your parents are very worried, they've asked me to take on your case. And I'm going to do that.'

Emily lay there feeling panic come into her mind like a rising tide. What was he talking about? She wasn't a case, she was a person, with a problem called Boggart. And so was Jessup.

'I shall be having some nice chats with your brother too,' said Dr Stigmore, as if he were reading her thoughts.

Emily's favourite nurse came bustling in, a round-faced, motherly woman with an Irish accent. She paused when she saw Dr Stigmore, and looked at him warily.

'Good evening, nurse,' he said, with an ingrati-ating smile, 'I'm Dr Stigmore from the psychiatric unit. Emily's a friend of mine.'

The nurse looked at Emily.

'My head hurts, nurse,' Emily said plaintively. 'It throbs when anyone makes a noise.'

The nurse looked back at Dr Stigmore, with an expression that said more clearly than words, *Out!*

He stood up hurriedly. 'Well, I must be off. I'll see you soon, Emily.'

'Is he really a friend of yours?' said the nurse, plumping Emily's pillow as the door closed.

'No,' Emily said.

'Doctors!' said the nurse witheringly. 'You don't need a shrink, you need a good night's sleep.'

Jessup was in bed, but he was not sleeping. He tossed to and fro, his mind jangling. The worry about Emily had grown less, once the doctor had reassured them – several times – that her only injuries were bruises, the broken ankle and the cracked rib. His larger worry, still growing, was the Boggart. Where was he? What would he do next? What would happen if he got into the underground, or an aeroplane – or a nuclear reactor? Jessup clung desperately to the memory of Willie saying, 'He'll go with you – he's a family fellow.' But what were they to do, with this creature let loose in a world where all his innocent tricks became disasters?

Like the irritating buzz of a fly, his mind kept showing him the image of the Boggart's dish of ice cream that afternoon. A little white mound of vanilla ice cream, gobbled up so fast that it was there one minute, gone the next. He tried to push the picture away – and then suddenly he knew why it was there. His mind was using it to jog him into remembering something else, something further away, back in Scotland. He remembered Tommy Cameron, in the kitchen of Castle Keep, talking about the MacDevon, after Emily had noticed he had no refrigerator, but only a pantry.

I guess Mr MacDevon didn't buy ice cream.

Once in a while he did – he was very fond of vanilla ice cream, and so was the dog.

Only Tommy hadn't said 'the dog' at first, not until after Jessup had jumped on the strange thing he had said instead.

'*He was very fond of vanilla ice cream, and so was the Bog–*'

The Boggart.

Tommy Cameron knew about the Boggart.

Jessup looked at his clock radio. It was two-fifteen in the morning. He had heard the murmur of talk until late, but his parents had been silent and presumably asleep for more than an hour now. He had pretended to be asleep himself the last couple of times they had looked in.

He lay wakeful and excited now, thinking about how to talk to Tommy Cameron.

Britain was five hours ahead of Ontario. He remembered that, from changing his watch when they reached London. That meant it was seven-fifteen in the morning now, in Port Appin. What was the Camerons' telephone number? He knew Emily had the address, written carefully in the little book he had given her last Christmas; though she was not a neat person, she was very good at making lists and filling out forms and such. It would be just like her to have written down the telephone number as well. Now if he could just find Emily's address book, in her untidy room . . .

Fifteen minutes later, in dressing gown and socks, he was shutting himself carefully, silently, into the kitchen, where the telephone would be safely inaudible from his parents' bedroom. The kitten, Polly, rubbed herself against his legs, delighted, purring. Very carefully, Jessup picked up the telephone and dialled.

'Hello, operator? I want to make a call to Scotland, please. And I need to find out how much it costs . . .'

When the ringing tone finally came at the other end it was echoing and old-fashioned, a truly bell-like sound, and suddenly Jessup was back in the crowded little shop, with the grey sky outside its window and the dark shape of Castle Keep lowering against the misty hills of Mull. After the third ring, Tommy's voice said clearly, 'Hello?'

'Thank goodness you're there,' Jessup said. 'I was afraid I'd wake your parents up. It's Jessup.'

There was a short astounded pause. 'Jessup! You just caught me, I'm off to school. I thought you were Angus Mackay wanting a book again. Where are you?'

'Toronto.'

'You sound as if you were next door.'

'It's fibre optics,' said Jessup, but science was not in the front of his head, for once. He took a breath. 'Tommy, this is urgent. You have to tell me about the Boggart.'

After another moment's pause Tommy said cautiously, 'Tell you what?'

'We've got him,' Jessup said. 'He's over here. He must have come with the furniture. He's making all sorts of trouble.'

'So that's it!' Tommy said. 'There's been no sign of him, I thought he was asleep.'

'Tell me!'

'He lives in the castle, he belongs with the MacDevon. Or he used to. He's a jokey fellow, but he means no harm. He doesn't speak. Animals know he's there but not people, generally. Only Mr MacDevon and me knew.'

'How do you control him? Stop him doing things?'

'You can't,' Tommy said. There was a blurry

noise in the background. 'I have to go, the car's here. The school bus.'

'We can't? Not at all?'

'He's an Old Thing, Mr MacDevon said, an Old Thing with capital letters – and they do what they want to do. They're outside the rules. They won't do anything unless it's what they want. Jessup, write to me, tell me what's happening.'

'OK,' Jessup said bleakly.

'There's one thing. They sleep a lot. For days, or weeks. Sometimes when you think he's not there, he's just asleep. I've got to go.'

'I'll write to you.'

'Love to Emily,' Tommy said, and he was gone.

Jessup put the phone down and sat staring at it. *They sleep a lot. For days, or weeks.* Perhaps for a while they could stop worrying about what the Boggart might be doing if he wasn't playing with furniture or lights. He rubbed Polly between the ears and put her back in her cat bed.

The telephone rang.

Jessup leaped at it in horror and caught it in the middle of the second ring. 'Hello?'

'Eleven-fifty,' said the operator's voice.

'Excuse me?'

'The cost of your call was eleven dollars and fifty cents. Have a nice night.'

'Oh. Thank you.'

He hung up, and yawned.

Up in Maggie and Robert's bedroom, Robert stirred and groaned as the telephone rang once, twice. Maggie reached a groggy arm over him towards the bedside table, but the ringing had stopped. Robert rolled over in bed, and tugged her arm down.

'Leave it,' he said, his voice thick with sleep, 'It's just that damn poltergeist.'

'But Emily isn't here,' Maggie said. 'She's the one who's supposed to be making those things happen.' She paused, concerned. 'D'you think Dr Stigmore is really right about that?'

There was no answer but heavy breathing. Robert was asleep again.

CHAPTER ELEVEN

'SO HE must be asleep somewhere,' Jessup said. 'In here, or in my room, or who knows where.'

'That's all very well until he wakes up.' Emily reached for another tissue and blew her nose. She had been shut up in the house for two days, having brought home from the hospital not only her plaster-encased leg and spectacular bruises but a ferocious cold in the head.

'"For days or weeks", Tommy said.'

'What else did he say?'

'Not much. I said we'd write and tell him everything. You could do that while I'm at school.' Jessup may have been a genius with figures and computer screens, but he was not fond of putting words together.

'Did he get my last postcard?'

'We didn't talk about you, we were talking about the Boggart.' Jessup paused, then relented. 'Well, he did say hi. When he rang off, he said, *Love to Emily.*'

Emily sat up straighter in bed. 'Did he really?'

Jessup crowed, and pointed a finger at her. 'You're blushing! Your face is all red!'

'My face is red because I have a fever of a hundred and two,' Emily said with dignity, lying down again. 'And if Mom catches you in here she'll have your ears off.'

'Bye. Send Tommy my love.' Jessup withdrew, grinning.

Emily lay contemplating the effort of writing a letter to Tommy Cameron, and decided against it. Her head ached as much from the stuffed-up effect of her cold as it had from being bashed against the road surface, and she felt miserable with worry. Everything was terrible. It had been bad enough having to cope with the Boggart, but now they had Dr Stigmore and his poltergeist theories as well. She thought despondently of telling her parents about the Boggart, and knew that it was too late: however much they loved her, they wouldn't be able to forget that a sensible helpful doctor was telling them she was creating all the Boggart disturbances herself. Though for Emily this seemed quite as difficult as believing in magic. How could the mind of a twelve-year-old girl make a big heavy sofa fly through the air?

She blew her nose again, and gave a miserable little moan.

'Oh, poor baby,' said Maggie sympathetically, coming through the bedroom door with a tray. 'You really don't deserve a cold as well. Here, I brought you some hot honey and lemon. And a babysitter for the afternoon.'

Emily looked over her shoulder, and saw Willie looming in the doorway. He nodded at her gravely.

'Good afternoon, Miss Volnik,' he said in his plummiest actor's voice.

'Oh, Willie!' said Emily. She was so glad to see him she felt she might cry.

'I know you're perfectly all right on your own,' Maggie said. 'But Willie stopped by, and he says he has a part to learn anyway, and I'd just feel happier if there's someone in the house. OK? I'll be at the shop if you need me.' She kissed Emily on the forehead, and then felt the forehead anxiously with her hand. 'Oh dear, you're still hot. Have you had an aspirin?'

Emily nodded.

'Stay in bed, now. I won't be late – it's supposed to snow.'

'Buzz off, Mags,' said Willie amiably. 'I'll take care of her.'

'You're an angel. Goodbye, loves.'

She was gone.

Willie sat down on the small chair beside Emily's bed. It creaked protestingly. He said, 'I came to warn you.'

'What about?' Emily said in alarm.

'There were a lot of people in the theatre the other day, when the Boggart was having his fling, and at least one of them has been talking. You know what a village this city can be, especially in our trade. Have you heard of a TV programme called *Beyond Belief*?'

Emily wrinkled her nose. 'Yeah, Mom watches it sometimes. It's a sort of documentary series, about flying saucers and stuff like that. I watched once, but it was really tacky.'

'Yes,' Willie said. 'The thinking man's *Believe It or Not*. Well, apparently they're working on a programme about ghosts, and someone from the Chervil has given them the idea that the theatre's haunted. So they keep hovering with a camera, even though Robert's told them to bug off.'

Emily gave a small wry smile. 'They'll have trouble filming the Boggart.'

Willie said grimly, 'They wouldn't have trouble filming his little tricks, if they happen across him. And then the place would go crazy, and Lord knows what he'd get up to. He goes where you go, Em – you're going to have to keep away from the theatre, and just pray the TV people don't come here.'

Emily's head began to ache even more. 'And the doctor,' she said.

'What doctor?'

'His name's Stigmore, he's a psychiatrist. Mom knows him. He says it's Jess and me making the Boggart things happen – he wants to study us.'

Willie snorted. 'Fellow's an imbecile.' He got up, and pulled a paperback from his pocket. 'Now I'm going to learn lines and you're going to have a sleep.'

'I'm not sleepy. Can I cue you?' Emily was an old hand at hearing actors rehearse their lines. On the rare occasions when her father acted, he took weeks to learn his words and was always convinced he was going to forget them.

'Yes, please,' said Willie promptly. But before he

could even hand her the book, there was a ring at the front doorbell.

'Ignore it,' Emily said.

'Better not. Might be your mother, forgot her key.' Willie went out, and shortly Emily heard the murmur of male voices from downstairs. When the voices didn't stop, but instead began to rise a little, she hauled her cast out of bed and put her head out of the bedroom door to listen.

'There is absolutely no question of that!' Willie was announcing stiffly, sounding like a nineteenth-century English butler. 'It's not my place to make such decisions.'

Rumble-rumble-rumble, went the other voice persistently. Whoever he was, he didn't have William Walker's powers of voice projection.

'Don't you understand, my good man – the child is sick!' Willie's voice said testily.

Rumble-rumble. Rumble-rumble.

'That's for Mrs Volnik to decide,' said Willie. 'Good afternoon!' The door slammed.

Emily hobbled back into bed just before Willie came puffing upstairs. 'Speak of the devil!' he said, now sounding his Scottish self again. 'That was your Dr Stigmore. Not a lovable man, not at all.'

'Jess and I call him the creep.'

'Very apt. He was insisting Maggie would like him to talk to you, so I sent him away with a flea in his ear. I think I'm going to make us both a cup of tea, to soothe the nerves.'

'Oh, Willie, I'm so glad you're here.' Emily said. She slid back under the covers again as he went downstairs, and lay there feeling safe and protected. It was a wonderful change from the nervous uncertainty that had become her normal state of mind since the Boggart first appeared. She closed her eyes, and the aspirin began to carry her headache away, and very soon she drifted into sleep.

Up on Emily's bookshelf the Boggart slept too, a long exhausted sleep unbroken since the day of his travels into the theatre light board and the city traffic lights. He didn't stir, not even when the sky outside grew thick and ominous, full of grey cloud, and the first snowflakes began to float down.

The snow fell for two days and nights, whirling in the wind that blew off Lake Ontario, muffling the trees and ravines of Toronto, turning the whole city white. It was the kind of storm that belonged normally to January, not November, and it was followed by what the weather forecasters called 'a frigid blast of Arctic air', which spread a murderous coating of ice over streets and pavements where the snow had been cleared. Most of the schools closed down, and a great many offices. Jessup had a happy time with the Gang of Five, dividing his days between the computer screen and the hockey rink. Emily rested. She read a lot. Her temperature went down and her bruises began to change to a remarkable shade of brownish-yellow, and she began to practise walking on crutches, though so far only on trips to the bathroom.

There was still no sign of the Boggart. Maggie was greatly relieved to find that the house, the shop and the theatre were all blessedly free of strange sounds or flying furniture, until Dr Stigmore suggested over the telephone that this was due only to the fact that Emily had been confined to bed.

Emily wrote to Tommy Cameron telling him all the details of the previous few weeks, but her letter crossed one from him. He sent her a fat envelope full of pictures of the Scottish Highlands and the Western Isles: postcards, photographs, pictures torn from calendars or magazines. They were wonderful images of misted purple mountains and grey-blue lochs and seas; there was a big, romantic picture of Castle Keep brooding dark and lonely on its rock, and an even bigger one of the seals, all wide dark eyes and bristling whiskers. Tommy wrote, 'I don't know what good it will do, but I think you should put these all over your bedroom walls. They might remind him of where he ought to be. The problem will be, how to persuade him to go there.'

Emily said to Jessup, 'And how would he go? Can you imagine what he'd do to a plane?'

Jessup said without much hope, 'D'you suppose any birds migrate from Canada to Scotland?'

They pinned up the pictures of Scotland all around Emily's room, so that the room began to look like a sort of small shrine to Scottishness. Maggie brought Robert in to look at it late one evening when Emily was asleep, and then took him back downstairs and asked if he thought they should be worried.

'Worried?' said Robert. 'They're great pictures. She liked Scotland. Why worry?'

'It's so sudden. And different. Dr Stigmore said we should tell him if either of them does anything different.'

'If you ask me, your friend Stigmore has an overactive imagination.'

Maggie said, 'You weren't in the shop when the furniture was flying around.'

'No,' said Robert, who had heard such highly coloured descriptions of this incident from Maggie and Dr Stigmore, each slightly different in detail, that he wasn't sure what he believed.

'And what about the things that happened when Em was at the theatre?' Maggie persisted. 'The lights going insane, and the computer.'

Robert said mildly, 'Computerized light boards aren't perfect, you know. They're a great modern advance until the day something goes wrong, and then it's not just a little mistake, it's a great screaming disaster.'

Maggie gave a doubtful sniff, and took the coffee cups out to the kitchen. Robert sat thinking wistfully of the magical lighting effects that had filled his stage that day. They were more hauntingly beautiful than any he had ever seen in the theatre. He had worked for hours with Phil the designer to try to reproduce some of them, but with no success. It was as if the effects were impossible to achieve without something more than the equipment the Chervil owned. Which was, of course, quite true.

The Boggart woke up on a bright morning when the temperature outside the house was several degrees below zero, Fahrenheit. The first thing that he saw, in the clear light filling the room, was the hypnotic array of photographs of Appin: his castle, his landscape and loch, his friends the seals.

He flittered from one picture to the next, filled suddenly with longing for the smell of the seaweed and the damp fallen leaves, for the soft salty air and the fine mist that was not quite rain; for draughty Castle Keep and the seagulls mewing around its roof. These pictures brought it all back to him, acutely vivid, and at the same time reminded him that he was in quite another place. The Boggart had very little sense of geography, and made no distinction between one place or country and another inside the North American continent. But he did know, as instinctively as a bird or any other wild thing, that he was on the other side of a very large ocean, a long way from home. And he was consumed by a desperate homesickness.

He flittered across to the window, and was startled by the whiteness. He had never seen snow so deep. It was mounded a foot high on the windowsills, against the glass, and the streets outside seemed all white and grey and black, with no colour anywhere. In banks and drifts the snow gleamed in the sunshine. Faintly he heard voices and laughter, and he saw Jessup and Chris chasing Barry down the pavement, throwing snowballs.

The Boggart's homesickness faded a little. He looked out at this crisp glittering world, fascinated. In the winters of his part of Scotland snow did not fall often, and it did not lie for long; only the mountaintops were white until spring. The snowy Toronto street beckoned him; he wanted to be out there, sharing the sunshine and the brilliant whiteness.

He flittered downstairs, hoping that someone might open a door. He had learned already that the Volniks' house, unlike Castle Keep, was tightly closed, with no cracks or crannies through which a boggart could come and go. The windows had not only one layer of glass, but two. These people seemed to be determined to keep out the good fresh air.

He hovered hopefully in the front hall, and in a little while his patience was rewarded; Jessup came bursting in, his face gleaming red, and disappeared into the bathroom. When he came out, the Boggart dived on to his shoulder, and sat there clutching the jacket collar for balance as Jessup ran outdoors again.

But it wasn't what he had expected at all. The shock nearly paralysed him. In an instant, the fiercely cold air sucked the energy out of his insubstantial, invisible body like a vacuum cleaner sucking out dust. Just as the Boggart had never seen deep long-lying snow, so he had never felt anything like the bitter cold of the Canadian winter; his coastal Scottish climate was gentle in comparison. Gasping for consciousness, he wound his long fingers in the fur edging of Jessup's hood, and with his last thread of strength managed to haul himself over the edge and down inside Jessup's shirt. Jessup wriggled, feeling the sudden prickle of cold – but then ducked to avoid a snowball, and forgot everything but the swift noisy compulsion to grab up his own handful of snow and send it whizzing back. He yelled in triumph as the snowball hit Barry's shoulder, and the Boggart winced as the noise of the yell flooded his chilly ears.

For the last ten minutes of the snow fight, the Boggart clung to the inside of Jessup's shirt, tucked in the gap above his collarbone. He was bounced around horribly every time the arm connected to the collarbone threw a snowball, but at least he was close to the warmth of Jessup's skin, protected from the terrible cold of the winter air outside. When at last the cold was too much even for the boys, and they came running back indoors shouting for mugs of hot chocolate, the Boggart squeezed himself out while Jessup was taking off his jacket, and he flittered feebly back upstairs.

He sat on the edge of Emily's bookshelf, gradually growing warmer again in the house shut so wisely against the bitter winter air, and he gazed quietly at the pictures of green Scottish hillsides for a long, long time.

Next day Jessup, Barry and Yung Hee spent an hour working on Black Hole, their computer game. Then they reached an impasse, and decided they needed a break. Yung Hee wandered into Emily's room to chat, and Jessup, still sitting at the computer, began bragging to Barry about a selection of new typefaces he had been illegally given by another computer-geek friend.

'They're much nicer than those big heavy sans serifs that shout at you. Look, here's my favourite, I'm using it for everything. It's more like Garamond.'

He clicked on a document whose icon was waiting on his computer's desktop, and instructed the computer to print it out. There were the usual whispered clicking and whirring sounds, and the printer gently spat out a piece of paper. Jessup took it out of the tray and handed it to Barry, grinning. 'It's a piece we're going to stick on the fridge to stop Mom smoking,' he said. 'Em found it – it comes from an old English book called *A Counterblast against Tobacco.*'

Barry read the sheet, frowned, and put it in front of Jessup.

'Don't you like it?' Jessup said, wounded. Then he paused, looking at the page. It read:

Smoking is a habit loathsome to the eye, hateful to the nose, harmful THA MI 'G IARRAIDH 'DOL DO'M DHUTHAICH FHEIN to the brain, dangerous to the lungs, and in the black stinking fumes thereof, THA MI 'GIARRAIDH 'DOL DO'M DHUTHAICH FHEIN nearest resembling the horrible Stygian smoke of the pit that is bottomless.

Barry said, 'Yeah, that's a pretty typeface, but where's the garbage coming from?'

Jessup frowned at the intrusive lines of capital letters. 'I never saw that before.'

'You think it's a virus?'

'Can't be. I've got top-of-the-line anti-virus on here. Nothing gets through.' He pressed several keys, and the computer obediently printed the anti-tobacco paragraph again – and the strange invading words THA MI 'G IARRAIDH 'DOL DO'M DHUTHAICH FHEIN were still there.

Jessup breathed heavily. His fingers spoke to the computer, and a little box with words inside appeared on the screen. 'Conducting virus scan on file TOBACCO,' it said. There was a flicker, and almost at once the words inside the little box changed. 'No viruses found during this scan!'

But before Jessup had even touched the keyboard again, the little box on the screen vanished, and in even bigger capitals than before they saw the same unintelligible words.

THA MI 'G IARRAIDH 'DOL DO'M DHUTHAICH FHEIN

'What's the matter?' Yung Hee said.

Jessup said, 'My computer's lost its mind.'

'Garbage in, garbage out,' said Emily. It was their father's favourite comment on the performance of computers and their operators.

Jessup snarled at her.

'Emily!' Maggie was at the bedroom door, looking concerned. 'I didn't know you were up. You shouldn't be roaming about on that leg.'

'I'm not on it.' Emily lifted a crutch and waggled it. 'I'm on these. The doctor said I could.'

'Just take it easy,' Maggie said. She moved a little sideways in the doorway, with a rather formal smile. 'Well, now you have another doctor visiting.'

Looming over her they saw the heavy dark eyebrows and forelock of Dr Stigmore. Emily's heart sank. She stood still, leaning on her crutches, hoping vaguely that if she stayed within the circle of her friends he might go away.

'Hello, Emily!' said Dr Stigmore, with the unconvincing heartiness she remembered from his hospital visit.

'Hello,' said Emily coldly.

'I brought you a present,' he said, and showed her a pot of yellow chrysanthemums. Emily was not fond of chrysanthemums; she thought they smelled like wet cats.

'Thank you very much,' she said without enthusiasm.

'Put them in your room, then,' said Maggie with a faint edge of impatience.

'No, no,' said Dr Stigmore. 'She's on crutches, poor child. I'll do it. Show me where, Emily.'

With a very bad grace, Emily hopped out of Jessup's room and across the landing to her own.

It was extremely untidy, and the bed unmade, but Dr Stigmore made elaborate comments on the prettiness of the curtains, and the originality of the drawings Emily had made on the wallpaper with a stolen Magic Marker when she was six.

From the curtain-rod, the Boggart looked down peevishly at Dr Stigmore. He recognized him. This was the man who had come bursting into Maggie Volnik's shop, interrupting the show he was putting on for Emily and Jessup. This man had spoiled his friends' fun, and his own. The Boggart felt a wave of dislike for him; he wanted him to leave, at once. He looked around for objects that might encourage the process.

From his room, the first shout Jessup heard came from Dr Stigmore. Then there was a loud crash, and a shriek from Maggie. Jessup, Yung Hee and Barry rushed through Emily's door just in time to see a large school textbook hurtle through the air and hit the wall, narrowly missing them. The carpet was covered with pieces of flowerpot, and spilled earth, and scattered yellow chrysanthemums. A shower of pencils rattled against the wall and fell on the broken flowers. Maggie was pressed back against the wall, looking terrified, and Dr Stigmore was dancing about the room, dodging the missiles, with a wild, excited grin on his face. 'Wonderful!' he was exclaiming. 'Classic! Wonderful!'

Emily was in a corner, wide-eyed, a crutch under each arm. She shouted, 'Stop it, Boggart! Stop!'

Another book whizzed through the air from the bookshelves. Instinctively Jessup ducked. Barry whooped, and tugged Yung Hee back out through the door. Dr Stigmore ducked too, but the book grazed his forehead before dropping to the ground. He staggered, and a bright trickle of blood appeared above his brow. Maggie wailed, aghast.

Suddenly there was silence. Emily glanced nervously around the room. She grabbed some tissues from a box on her dressing table and handed them to Dr Stigmore. He inclined his head in dignified thanks and dabbed gingerly at the graze on his forehead.

Maggie said faintly, 'Are you all right? Oh dear, I'm so sorry!'

Dr Stigmore's square, perfect white teeth gleamed at her. He looked like a large predatory animal about to gobble someone up. 'Quite remarkable,' he said happily. 'Amazing manifestations. It's so very uncommon to be able to conduct this kind of research. I can't wait to see what we find when we take Emily into the psychiatric unit for observation.'

Emily was horrified. She moved back towards Maggie as if for shelter. 'Mom!' she said.

Maggie looked uncertainly at Dr Stigmore. 'There surely isn't any reason for that?' she said.

Barry stuck his head cautiously around the door. 'Wow, Em!' he said. 'How do you do that?'

'It wasn't me!' Emily said, desperate.

Dr Stigmore said briskly to Maggie, 'Oh, there's no alternative. Dr Rhine's work in parapsychology showed conclusively that an evaluation of psychokinesis requires close, detailed study, under controlled conditions. It's very important to be able to rule out the possibility of manipulation, either by the subject or some dominating personality.'

Maggie Volnik was not the kind of woman to be cowed by long words. She said calmly, 'Perhaps you would repeat that in English.'

Dr Stigmore's black eyes narrowed. He said, 'In other words, if you want these disturbances to end, Emily needs to be watched day and night in a hospital.'

CHAPTER TWELVE

BARRY AND Yung Hee sat in Jessup's room, gaping at him in amazement. He had just finished telling them about the Boggart, and the background given them by Willie and Dai and Tommy Cameron.

'But creepy old Stigmore doesn't know anything about boggarts,' said Jessup. 'And he wouldn't believe it if he did. *He* thinks all these things are being thrown about by a poltergeist, which he says is a fancy name for energy coming out of a disturbed kid. In this case Emily.'

'Emily,' said Yung Hee, 'is about the least disturbed person I know.'

'Right. At least till now.'

They all fell silent for a moment, thinking of

the loud sobs with which Emily had greeted Dr Stigmore's continued insistence on her going into hospital. They had all retreated, quietly and quickly, and Dr Stigmore and Maggie were still shut up with Emily in her room. Jessup was concerned about her, but not distressed; he knew his sister very well, and had heard a note in those sobs that told him they were at least partly calculated. Emily was on the defensive, working out a strategy as she went along.

'Boggarts,' said Barry reflectively, as if he were trying the word out.

'There is a spirit a little like that in Korea,' Yung Hee said. 'I forget the name, but I have heard my grandmother tell. It lives in the house, and plays tricks.'

Barry said, 'This is really crazy. If I hadn't seen those books flying around –'

'You saw things flying around on Halloween,' Jessup said.

'Yeah, but I thought you guys had rigged that somehow. And you let me think it.'

'Well, it was only that night that we found out about the Boggart.' Jessup thought of the small invisible hand stroking his cheek, cool as the hand of a frog.

'Is he in here?' Yung Hee's shiny black hair

swung as she looked around the room, half fascinated, half fearful. 'Can he hear us?'

'Maybe.'

Barry stood up. 'We have to do something, quick. Before that jerk takes Emily away and starts sticking electrodes on her head.'

'Listen,' Jessup said. He glanced cautiously at the door, but it was still shut. 'When you go home, call Willie Walker for me. It'll be hard to phone from here. Ask him to come over tomorrow, if he can.'

'What can Willie do?'

'I don't know. But he's the only person we can ask.'

The door opened, and Maggie stood there alone, looking at them. 'Don't disturb Emily,' she said. 'She's going to sleep now.'

Jessup said, 'You aren't going to let him take her away?'

'No. Not yet, anyway.'

'Not ever!'

'Oh, Jessup,' Maggie said wearily, 'you really don't know what you're talking about. It's complicated.' She turned to Barry and Yung Hee. 'We have troubles in this family, as you see,' she said stiffly. 'I'd be grateful if you wouldn't speak about them to anybody.'

'Of course not!' said Yung Hee warmly. She darted forward and gave Maggie a kiss on the cheek.

Barry remained still. He said, 'You mean me, don't you? You've never trusted me.'

'I mean you and Yung Hee and Jess,' Maggie said.

'But especially me, because I'm a junkie and a bum and a bad influence. And all those other things you said at Halloween.'

Maggie said coolly, 'I think you're wasting your life by leaving school, but that's your problem. I'd just be grateful if you wouldn't discuss ours, outside this house.'

Barry shrugged. 'OK,' he said.

Jessup was furious with his mother; he glared at her, but she seemed to look through him. 'Dinner in half an hour, Jessup.' And she was gone.

'Stay cool, Jess,' Barry said. 'She's just worried. C'mon, Yung Hee – we're outa here.'

There was a loud crash downstairs, as Dr Stigmore opened the door to leave and the Boggart threw a vase at him.

The night was clear and cold, and the street lights cast harsh black shadows on the dingy white snowbanks edging the pavements. From the landing window, the Boggart tried to look up, to see the friendly prickle of the stars in the dark sky, but trees and buildings enclosed him and there were no stars to be seen. The house was sleeping, and he could not get outside; and even if he could, no creature would be stirring out there. It was too cold.

The Boggart was lonely.

He could play tricks, of course. Right this moment, he could make the sound of a howling wolf, or a clanking chain, or moan heartrendingly like a textbook ghost. His two friends might appreciate that, but nobody else in this house would, not even that hostile cat. They would call in the tall dark man, who was an enemy; who reacted to boggart games with a fierce self-satisfaction that made the Boggart very uneasy.

He flittered into Emily's room, and in the light that crept around the blind from the street lights outside, he gazed longingly at the pictures of the mountains of Argyll, and the rocks where the seals lived, and he wished that he were there.

Emily woke up with a sense of awful dread. It was as if she were being warned that something bad was about to happen. She lay unhappily in bed, in the morning light, drifting in and out of a kind of waking nightmare in which Dr Stigmore locked her in a room full of furniture and sat facing her, staring, waiting for tables and chairs to start flying about. And nothing moved, so they sat there for days, and days ... and outside, the Boggart was loose, playing his tricks, and Toronto caught fire and the whole of Canada lost its electricity, and aeroplanes crashed and ships went aground and nuclear power stations blew up ...

She shook herself awake and got dressed, more slowly than usual because of the cast on her leg. She heard a murmur of voices in Jessup's room, and then Robert came in and announced that Maggie had left early for Quebec on a buying trip, and that Jessup had every sign of the flu and would be staying in bed instead of going to school.

'The younger generation is falling apart,' he said. 'Are you well enough to get his lunch, if he wants any?'

'Sure,' said Emily. She was sorry for Jessup, but greatly relieved that the Boggart would not be shadowing him to school. Almost in the same moment she realized that the flu was probably due to Jessup's having had the same thought. They had a day together: one day, to solve the many-sided problem of the Boggart. Whatever could they do?

Robert said awkwardly, 'I hear last night was difficult.'

'Do you think I'm crazy?' demanded Emily.

'Nobody thinks you're crazy, Em. We're just looking for solutions to a very peculiar problem.'

Suddenly Emily just wanted to get rid of him. She loved her parents dearly, but they were out of their element in this situation, and it was urgent to get advice from someone with the right kind of understanding. Which meant someone Robert and Maggie would never dream of asking for advice.

She said, trying to sound calm, 'Jess and I will be fine.'

'I have a board meeting,' Robert said. He made a face. She could tell that in spite of the unstable condition of his family, his mind was already busy in the theatre. *Good*, she thought.

'Good luck, Dad.'

Robert departed, scarcely recognizable with a tie round his neck and a briefcase in his hand, and in a flash Jessup was out of bed and pulling on his clothes. He came down to join Emily in the kitchen, tugging a sweatshirt over his head. 'I did a truly excellent impersonation of a sick kid,' he said with satisfaction. 'I think I'll try out for the school play in the spring.'

Emily leaned on her crutches, worried, feeling quite unlike a reliable older sister. 'Oh, Jess,' she said plaintively. 'What are we going to do?'

'Stay indoors. He doesn't go out except with one of us.' Jessup spooned a dollop of home-made apple sauce into a bowl and poured cereal over it.

'That's no help. We can't stay indoors forever.'

'Maybe he won't do any more bad stuff like the traffic lights. After seeing what happened.'

'I bet he will. He just thinks it's fun.' Hovering near the table, the Boggart smiled. The girl was beginning to understand him. But he was more interested in the apple sauce than the conversation; he dipped one long finger into it, tasted, and shivered with pleasure. The kitchen had become his favourite room in the house; at least here he could be distracted by food, and forget that he was in the wrong country, the wrong place.

The telephone rang. Emily picked it up.

'Hello?'

'Hi,' said a warm, friendly voice. 'Mrs Volnik?'

'No, this is Emily.'

The voice sounded delighted. 'Emily! This is Mary Brogan of Eastern Television. I work for a programme called *Beyond Belief.* I understand you've been having some interesting, er, manifestations recently.'

'No!' said Emily in a panic. 'No, we haven't!'

The voice was calm and persistent. 'Furniture being thrown about, and books. And strange lights shining in your father's theatre. Isn't that right?'

'No!' said Emily. She put the phone down hastily.

'Someone selling something?' Jessup said, through a mouthful of cereal.

'Sort of.'

The doorbell rang. Emily jumped.

'I'll go,' said Jessup.

'Don't let anyone in!'

'Don't worry.' He pushed back his chair and went out, and the Boggart sat down happily on the rim of his cereal bowl and drank the remaining small pool of milk. Very faintly, Emily heard the slurping sound; it was like a dripping tap. She was about to get up and check the sink when Willie came into the room.

'Willie!' She fumbled happily for her crutches, and Willie put a large hand on her shoulder to keep her in the chair.

'Hello, Em,' he said. 'Nice to see you vertical again.'

'Did Jessup tell you –'

'I've heard. Not content with getting you knocked down by a bus, our friend has been throwing things about again. I'd like to have a word with your boggart.'

The Boggart flittered up to a shelf and regarded Willie with wary interest. Here was a man of experience, with a voice that sounded strangely familiar.

'Where is he?' said Willie. He was a large man, and standing there he seemed to fill the kitchen.

'Who knows?' Emily said despondently. 'Up in one of our bedrooms, I guess. He sleeps a lot.'

'Just as well,' said Willie. 'Come on, then.' They trooped upstairs. The Boggart forgot about Willie and dived happily at the apple sauce, which Jessup had forgotten to put back in the refrigerator.

Willie stood in the middle of Emily's bedroom and spoke to the ceiling. 'Are you there, then, my laddie?'

Silence.

Emily said, 'You only find that out if he doesn't like you, because then he throws something.'

'No harm in asking,' Willie said. He ambled into Jessup's room, and asked the same question.

There was silence. Again Emily and Jessup stood in the doorway, listening nervously for some sound of irritation or mischief.

Willie glanced down at the desk, where the computer screen glowed a muted silver. He paused for a moment, looking at a litter of papers; then he picked up the top sheet; then he sat down, staring at it.

'Jessup,' he said in an odd, tight voice, 'what's this?'

Jessup looked over his shoulder, and saw his tobacco quotation, with the repeated invading capitals THA MI'G IARRAIDH 'DOL DO'M DHUTHAICH FHEIN. 'Oh, that's just some stuff I was printing out to show someone a typeface. It got screwed up, I don't know how. There's some garbage in there.'

'That's not garbage,' Willie said, in the same strange voice. 'That's Gaelic.' He read the words aloud, and they sounded quite different from the way they looked on the page.

'Gaelic? Do you speak Gaelic?'

'Of course he does,' Emily said. 'He's Scottish.'

Willie said absently, 'It doesn't follow. But yes, I do.' He was still staring at the page.

'What does it mean, then?'

Willie looked up at them. 'It means, "*I want to go to my own country*".'

*

Willie stood by the front door, pulling on his parka and looking worried. He had spent a long time speaking Gaelic into the air, and typing it into the computer, in an attempt to communicate with the Boggart, but there had been no response, and now it was time for the matinee of *Cymbeline* at the Chervil.

He said, 'Call me at the theatre if anything happens, anything at all.'

'Thank you, Willie.'

Willie shook his shaggy head mournfully. 'I wish your boggart were more talkative.'

Hearing his name spoken in the warm Scottish accent, the Boggart came flittering out of the kitchen, interested, wiping a smear of apple sauce from his face. But the door had closed; Willie was gone.

Emily said desperately, 'Now what do we do?'

'I'm not going to budge from the computer,' Jessup said. 'It's the only way he's ever talked to us – I think he'll do it again.'

'In Gaelic? We shan't know what he's saying.'

'I don't care if it's in Martian, so long as it's *something*,' Jessup said. 'Anyway he obviously understands English, even if he isn't speaking it.' He headed for the stairs.

The Boggart flittered after him. He fancied a nap on Emily's bookshelf, after his apple-sauce snack.

Outside the house a car was parked at the edge of the street, with its engine running, and a woman sitting in the driver's seat. She spoke to Willie through the open window as he came by.

'Excuse me, Mr Volnik – I'm from Eastern Television –'

'Go away,' Willie said. He kept walking.

The car edged along beside him. 'You're not Mr Volnik, though, are you – you're one of the actors. William Walker – that's it! Mr Walker, I'm Mary Brogan of *Beyond Belief* –'

Willie paused, and gave her a beatific smile. 'Far, far beyond,' he said. 'Good afternoon.' And he slipped behind her car, crossed the road and disappeared down an alley too narrow for automobiles.

Mary Brogan snorted disdainfully, backed her car up and sat looking greedily at the Volniks' house.

Jessup sat at the computer keyboard, typing.
Boggart, come talk to us.
Boggart, where are you?
Boggart, it's your turn.

He took his hands from the keyboard and held them out, palms up, appealing.

Emily stood behind him anxiously, leaning on her crutches. 'He wants to go back to Scotland. He said he did. We should be thinking of ways to get him there.'

'That comes next. First we have to talk to him.'

'Couldn't he go back the way he came? He must have been inside one of the crates, with my desk or your table. There was no sign of him till after they arrived.'

'Em,' Jessup said. 'We can't do anything till we can reach him. You think you can open a little box and say, *OK, Boggart, jump in!* – and then just drop it in the mail?'

Emily said without conviction, 'Well, maybe.'

'Do me a favour!' Jessup said. He began playing with the keyboard again.

Emily sighed. 'I'll go make us some lunch. Peanut butter and jam?'

'I've gone off it,' Jessup said. 'Tuna fish.'

The Boggart flittered past the landing window on his way to Emily's room, and paused, staring out. Very faintly he could hear a sound that caught at his heart, carrying him instantly back to the grey waters and the rocky shore of Loch Linnhe. And then he saw them, out in the sky, high over the snowy treetops: seagulls, wheeling, drifting, calling their plaintive familiar cry. These were not the seagulls of the Hebrides; they were the gulls of Lake Ontario, who lived as much on Toronto rubbish as on fish, and they were not even the same kind of gull that flies over Scotland. But the Boggart did not know that. They were seagulls; their voices were calling him home.

Yet again he flittered into Emily's room and gazed longingly at the pictures of the seals on their rocks, the misty islands, and bleak, lonely Castle Keep. The MacDevon was not there any more; he was dead. Here in this curious, exciting new world, his new friends Emily and Jessup were alive. But this was not home for an Old Thing, nor ever would be. The Boggart knew what he must do. He looked at the laughing photograph of Emily and Jessup throwing snow at each other, and he reached out the long fingers of his insubstantial hand and gently touched each laughing face. Then he turned away. With his keen ageless ears, he listened for the faint hum of the computer, and he flittered out of Emily's room and in through Jessup's door.

*

Emily was halfway down the stairs, swinging between the crutches, when she heard Jessup's yell. With some difficulty she turned around and hopped upstairs again as fast as she could. Her ribs were beginning to ache.

Jessup was staring at the computer screen, his fingers motionless on the keyboard. He said huskily, 'Look!'

Emily looked. She saw the starry sky that was the usual background for the Gang of Five's computer game, Black Hole; it was patterned with constellations, striped by the bright path of the Milky Way. Black Hole was a game of space exploration; though she had never learned its details she knew they involved travelling in a spaceship to other planets, other galaxies. The players explored new worlds, fought off hostile aliens, but their greatest aim was to solve the mystery of Black Holes, those sinks of gravity into which all nearby matter would be sucked and utterly transformed. And their greatest danger was that a Black Hole itself would suck them in, before they could solve its mystery.

She saw the usual tiny spaceship which Jessup was controlling on the screen, moving steadily through space, and she wondered what she was supposed to be looking at, that he found so remarkable. Then she saw it. Something moved across the screen, more rapidly than the little ship. It was intensely bright, brighter than anything she had ever seen on a computer screen before, and it looked for all the world like an arrow of blue flame. Uncannily like the blue flames that had danced along the tram wires, or around the traffic lights, when the Boggart had gone on his downtown Toronto rampage.

'What a wonderful colour!' she said, entranced. 'How do you do it?'

'I'm not doing it,' Jessup said. 'I never saw it before. I don't know what's happening.' His eyes were wide and startled, fixed on the bright blue flame running just ahead of his spaceship icon into the depths of computer-simulated space. He said, 'I went on asking the Boggart to come use the computer again, to talk to me. But there were no words, he didn't type in anything. He wasn't here. So I thought I'd give up for a while, and I pulled up the game instead. And suddenly there was *this*.'

'I love it,' Emily said. 'You mean he's playing your game with you, only you're using a spaceship and he's using a blue flame.'

'No,' Jessup said unhappily. 'I mean he's *inside* my game. *That blue flame is the Boggart.*'

'He's inside your computer game?' Emily said, incredulous. 'That's impossible.'

'Of course it is. Everything about the Boggart is impossible.' Jessup was watching the blue flame, tracking it on the screen. 'But if you think about it, a computer is all electrical impulses and I suppose the Boggart is too. He's not solid, you can't see him or hear him or feel him.'

'We've heard him, once or twice. Noises. And we felt his hand.'

'Yes, we did. But that was because he wanted us to.' Jessup was quiet for a moment, remembering. Then he tensed, and on the screen Emily saw the blue flame approaching the lumpy moving shape of a small asteroid.

'What's that?'

'Asteroid. It could blast him to pieces.'

'Jess!'

'Well, but he's real – I don't see how it – well, let's fix that.' Jessup pressed buttons, and out of his spaceship icon, near the blue flame on the screen, a small rocket rushed at the asteroid. Both it and the asteroid disappeared. The blue flame bounced gaily up and down, as if it were dancing a jig.

'This is a very tough game,' Jessup said unhappily. 'I don't think he's taking it seriously. And he doesn't know the rules. He's heading on a course that's going to get awfully close to a black hole.'

'Can't you show him?' Emily gazed anxiously at the screen, wishing she knew more about computers.

'I can't talk to him. I can only try to nudge him away from dangerous things, so long as my spaceship's magnetic field's stronger than his. That's something we built in, we call it the buddy rule.' Jessup sent his spaceship diagonally across the screen, to head off the arrow of blue flame in a different direction. But the spaceship seemed to bounce against the invisible barrier, falling back and tumbling through space, and the blue flame danced its joyful little jig once more. Even as a blip on a computer screen, the Boggart was still delighting in mischief.

Jessup groaned. 'Oh, Boggart, *stop*!' he said. He rescued the tumbling spaceship icon and aimed it again at the speeding blue flame – and again and again the spaceship fell away, spinning helplessly, and the flame ran on across the screen.

Emily said, 'What about those Black Hole characters you used at Halloween? Ice Death, Fire Burst. Can't you use them to head him off somehow?'

'No way,' Jessup said. 'They live on one of the other planets. And he's out travelling through deep space.'

'Oh,' said Emily. She stood propped on her crutches, looking nervously over his shoulder.

Jessup became very silent and intent. He sat hunched over the keyboard, working furiously. But the moving flame could not be stopped; it sped on, faster and faster, driven by some huge determination of its own. Watching, Emily saw that the stars prickling in the black sky of the screen were beginning strangely to quiver, as if they were vibrating in some intense wave of sound. Gradually they seemed to blur, and grow faint, and all the time the blue arrow of flame raced deeper into space.

Suddenly Jessup sat back in his chair, his face pale. His hand dropped limp beside the keyboard. He said in an anguished whisper, 'It's the black hole – he's going into it! I can't stop him!'

And all at once the screen was filled by a dark, glimmering, pulsating whirlpool, a hole of ferocious energy pulling every thread of light into its dead black heart, and the blue flame dived into the centre and disappeared.

CHAPTER THIRTEEN

EMILY AND Jessup stared at the computer screen in horror. The dark whirlpool filled it, throbbing, like a living picture of death. Jessup jabbed frantically at different combinations of keys on the keyboard, but nothing changed. The black hole hung there, dreadful, unchanging, empty.

'Get him back! Jess, get him back!'

'I can't!' Jessup said, desperate. 'We didn't programme recovery into the game! If you fell into the black hole you were gone, wiped out. That was it.'

'I thought this game was supposed to be all about discovering what black holes are?'

'It is, but we haven't got that far yet. They still eat everything before we can figure out how they work.'

'It *can't* have eaten the Boggart! He's not part of the game! Where is he?'

'I don't know!'

They stared at each other, distraught. Tears prickled in Emily's eyes. She was desperate to see the Boggart again; she couldn't bear to think of his being harmed. Whatever he had done to their lives, she loved his sense of mischief, his liveliness, his communication of delight. He was a nuisance, but he was their friend.

She turned on Jessup. 'I hate your stupid computer and its games!' she shrieked.

Jessup's lip quivered; suddenly he was only an anxious small boy. 'It was the only way he could talk to us . . .'

Downstairs, a door slammed, and Robert's voice shouted cheerfully, 'Hi, kids! How're you feeling? My meeting was cancelled – I'll make you Volnik salad for lunch.'

The day became an endless suspended nightmare. Robert had brought with him a briefcase full of papers so that he could work at home instead of at the theatre. Moved by his children's ailments, he was determined to be a good devoted father – hence the Volnik salad, which was a family favourite seldom prepared because it involved so many finely chopped vegetables. Emily drooped over her crutches in the kitchen, keeping him company while he chopped away gaily on the chopping board. She thought of Jessup upstairs, supposedly lying in the grip of the symptoms of flu, but in fact trying desperately to invent some way of combating the Black Hole.

Robert reached for a stalk of celery. 'Is Jess asleep?'

'I think so.'

'Poor kid. He sounded knocked out. There's a miserable flu bug going around.'

Emily shifted on her crutches until she was standing between Robert and the telephone. She had noticed a small red light flashing on the phone: the sign that someone was using an extension elsewhere in the house. It wouldn't do for a knocked-out flu victim to be found frantically making complex technical telephone calls to his computer friends.

But none of Jessup's telephone calls – made at nerve-racking intervals during the afternoon, whenever Robert was occupied somewhere out of reach of a phone – brought him any help. Yung Hee, reached on her mobile phone after a school orchestra rehearsal, called back with several suggestions, including one from her Korean grandmother about the casting of a spell, but became discouraged the third time Robert answered the phone and told her Jessup was not taking calls. Chris, reached later still after a hockey practice, could not understand Jessup's concern about anything consumed by a black hole, since he hadn't been told about the Boggart and Jessup hadn't the heart to start explaining the story now. Barry's telephone did not answer. The technician at the local computer store had no ideas because, as he reasonably pointed out to Jessup, the rules of a private computer game were known only to those who had devised the game in the first place.

And Jessup and his friends had not thought to invent rules covering the behaviour of an invading Boggart in their Black Hole game.

Jessup lay in bed that evening, staring across the room at his computer screen. His mother was home now, full of tales about furniture deals in Quebec. She had brought him his supper, and expressed satisfaction that he had no fever. Then she approached the computer, which now showed the squiggles and twirls of Jessup's favourite screen-saver program, an abstract pattern of colours which he alternated sometimes with the peaceful image of a drifting school of fish. The instant Jessup's fingers were back on the keyboard, these twirls would vanish and the screen would fill once more with the shadowy depths of the black hole.

Maggie reached a hand to the computer and glanced at Jessup. 'Why don't I turn this off?'

'No!' Jessup flung back the bedclothes and was across the room in an instant, like some fierce maternal creature protecting her young. He grabbed Maggie's wrist.

His startled mother looked down at him. 'Jess, are you crazy? Go back to bed! I get the message, I won't turn it off.'

'Swear!' said Jessup.

'I swear. Good grief.'

'Especially when I'm asleep. Swear you won't turn it off while I'm asleep.'

'*Go back to bed!*' said Maggie, her voice rising ominously.

Jessup climbed back into bed. He said tremulously, 'There's something very important I don't want to lose.'

'Don't worry,' said his mother more gently. She stroked his hair. 'I won't touch it. Just go to sleep, love.'

But Jessup didn't sleep. He lay there for hours, staring at the glimmering screen, thinking about the Boggart, trying to imagine where in his computer the Boggart could possibly be. Again and again he went through, in his head, the rules and pattern they had devised for the game of Black Hole. He longed to be able to talk to Barry, who had all along been his chief collaborator in the making of the game. Barry had more experience and understanding of computers than anyone in the Gang of Five; he was more likely than any of them to come up with some original and off-beat idea. But Barry was not answering his mobile phone, which he often ignored, and it was far too late now to call his house. Jessup thought wistfully of the night when he had lain awake and been able to telephone Tommy Cameron, because of the five-hour time difference. In Barry's house, unfortunately, it was just as late as it was in his own.

But then he remembered the shape of Barry's house. It was a Victorian mansion with many rooms, including two separate and enormous studies for Barry's father, a world-famous management consultant, and Barry's mother, who had a belligerently different surname and was vice president of a bank. Attached to the mansion was a carriage house. Its ground floor housed the present-day carriages, the mother's Mercedes and the father's Jaguar, and above them was a studio. This studio was Barry's bedroom, and nobody would hear his mobile phone – if he answered it.

Jessup crept downstairs to the kitchen, stroked the cat, closed the door and dialled Barry's number. There was a great deal of ringing and then a very blurry voice. 'H'lo?'

'Barry? It's Jessup.'

'For Pete's sake – it's three in the morning!'

'I know it is,' Jessup said, and to his horror he suddenly found his voice full of tears. 'I know it is. I'm sorry. Oh, Barry, I've lost the Boggart.'

'Lost him?'

Jessup told him the story, and all the while he was fighting to keep his voice from shamefully breaking, for like Emily, he had discovered he was fiercely attached to their invisible, tiresome, uninvited friend. Being himself a good friend, Barry was aware of this, and when Jessup had finished he said simply, 'I'll be there in twenty minutes.'

'Thanks,' Jessup said gratefully.

'You got an alarm system?'

'They don't put it on when we're home.'

'I'll tap at your kitchen door.'

Quietly and carefully Jessup made two mugs of hot chocolate. He gave a splash of milk to Polly the cat, who could hardly believe her luck and purred so loudly he was afraid she would wake his parents up. In a little while he heard a strange scuffling outside the door, and opened it to find Barry, red-faced, shaking thick snow from his jacket and cap.

'More snow!' said Jessup, in a wondering whisper.

'It's been snowing for three hours, they haven't ploughed yet. I came on skis.'

'On *skis*?'

'My car's blown its silencer – makes a noise like a tank. I didn't think your mom would appreciate that, in the middle of the night.' Barry gulped his hot chocolate with enthusiasm, but his mind, as usual, was focused on computers. He said, 'I was wondering – your autosave is set for five minutes, right?'

'You bet.'

Barry reached down and began unlacing his boots. 'Let's get to that computer and try something . . .'

They crept upstairs, Jessup directing Barry to avoid the fourth stair from the top, which contained an abominable creak. Past his parents' bedroom, from which he heard reassuring sounds of regular breathing; up the last stairs, past Emily's almost-closed door. From Jessup's room came the faint, husky hum of his computer.

Jessup carefully closed his door, and Barry sat down at the desk like a pianist facing the start of a concerto. He took a deep deliberate breath. 'OK,' he said. 'Here we go.'

For more than two hours he worked at the computer, delving back into the process by which they had constructed the game of Black Hole; trying to reach the area into which the Boggart had disappeared. This was the thing he most loved doing: focusing all his mind on one thing, free from all outside complications and opinions. Now, though, like Jessup, he was driven too by panic. He trawled page after page of the game, frantically scanning the vast jumbled array of codes and numbers for a trace of the lost Boggart.

But Barry was hunting for more than codes or numbers; his quarry was alive. And it was not simply lost – it might also be deliberately eluding him. He and Jessup both knew there was a strong chance that the Boggart, always a creature of mischief, might be playing a terrible game of his own, not understanding that there were perils in the world of a computer from which even he might not be able to escape. If he was playing hide-and-seek with them, he might at any moment doom himself to go on playing it forever.

Barry sat with his long frame hunched over the keyboard, sometimes typing furiously, sometimes brooding, staring at the screen. Now and then Jessup took over, to try an idea of his own, but most of the things Barry was doing were so complex and obscure that it was impossible to help him. Again and again they tried to reconstruct the game in which, somewhere, the Boggart was hiding or trapped. But every time they failed.

The door opened, and Jessup swung around, alarmed. It was Emily, in her dressing gown, blinking sleepily.

'Barry!' she said in a startled whisper. 'What are you doing here?'

'Shut the door!' Jessup whispered. 'We're trying to find the Boggart!'

Barry stood up and stretched, touching the ceiling. He said gloomily, 'And it may be impossible.'

'Oh!' Emily said wretchedly. She sat down on Jessup's bed.

'Well, we've been trying for two hours.' Barry looked at his watch. 'No, three.' He seated himself at the computer again. 'Jess – I think there's only one thing left to do.'

Jessup said nervously, 'What's that?'

'Reverse the final info loop on the game and just see what happens.' He looked across at Emily. 'Roughly speaking, that means we go down the black hole too.'

'*Down the black hole?*'

'But that's a major recursive loop!' Jessup said.

'Right. Megamajor.'

'The computer will crash!'

'Maybe. On the other hand, we might find ourselves face to face with the Boggart.'

Emily said fearfully, 'What are you guys talking about? What does it mean if the computer crashes?'

'You have to restart it, and you lose what you've been working on. In our case, this Black Hole game – and the Boggart inside it.'

'You lose it *forever*?'

'Yup,' Barry said.

'Don't do it!' said Emily in panic.

Barry said, persistent, 'We've lost the Boggart anyway – nothing we've tried has been able to reach him. This is the only thing left. I think we have to try it. Take the risk.'

'So do I,' Jessup said.

Emily looked doubtfully at Barry: at the lanky sixteen-year-old frame, and the face that didn't quite seem to know yet what shape it was going to to be. Barry's long dark hair lay greasily over his shoulders, and his upper lip looked vaguely dirty because it needed a shave. He had a major acne pimple on his chin. He looked the image of the dubious layabout that Maggie Volnik thought him to be. But on that point Emily had always felt her mother was wrong.

Barry said gently, 'Em, I wouldn't do you dirt. Jess is just about my best friend, whatever your mom may feel about that. I really think this is what we have to do.'

'Mom doesn't mean any harm,' Emily said.

'She's all right,' Barry said. 'I like her. At least she cares what her kids do with their lives.'

'Let's do it!' Jessup nudged Barry's shoulder impatiently.

Emily nodded, her eyes on Barry's. 'OK.' She got up and hopped over to stand behind their chairs.

Barry turned back to the screen, and ran one

hand through his hair nervously. 'Down the black hole!' he said.

His fingers moved on the keyboard, and the screen was filled with the black sky and the prickling stars of the Black Hole game. There was no small spaceship icon visible in this sky, because now it was as if Jessup, Emily and Barry were inside the spaceship, and the computer screen was their window on space. They watched, and watched, and they seemed to move through space with agonizing slowness, for lack of reference points to show their speed. One star moved off the screen and out of sight; then another. Then a notice flashed, in a rectangle set in the centre of the starry screen.

CHECK YOUR COURSE!
DANGER!
CHECK YOUR COURSE!

Barry ignored the message, and instructed the computer to move on. Stars drifted gradually towards them through the dark sky, giving an eerily vivid illusion that they were indeed looking through the window of their own spaceship. Then the computer began to make a high bleeping sound, and a second warning flashed.

DANGER!
YOU ARE NEARING BLACK HOLE!
CHANGE YOUR COURSE!

Barry turned off the warning and the sound alarm. They travelled on in silence. But gradually Emily thought she began to see a strange quivering in the sky, as she had when the Boggart's cheerful blue arrow of flame was streaking towards disaster. It grew stronger, until the stars on the screen were no longer still points of light but small juddering scribbles, jerking up and down. The sense of vibration consumed Emily's consciousness until she felt as if the floor under her feet were shaking; as if she were truly inside a doomed spaceship. Propped on her crutches, she grabbed Barry's shoulder with one hand and Jessup's arm with the other, as huge letters on the screen flared a final warning at them:

DANGER!!!
DANGER!!!
DANGER!!!

And the screen filled again with the whirling, pulsing dark funnel that was the black hole, sucking them down, and they felt that in a terrifying giddy fall they plunged into its black centre, the heart of death, taking their breath, taking all light from their eyes, all sound from their ears. Jessup closed his eyes, knowing this was the moment when his computer would crash, when its screen would turn black and dreadful noises rattle deep inside its calm grey body, and when everything that had been fed by its energy would be lost. Including the Boggart.

But instead he heard a gasp of wonder from Emily.

He opened his eyes, and on the screen of his computer he saw Castle Keep.

It was a clear, beautiful image, far clearer than any picture normally generated by a computer or even a film camera. It swayed a little, as though they were looking at it from a boat. A seagull swept across the screen, calling its discordant, plaintive cry, and suddenly Jessup felt that he was indeed in a boat, tossing gently, looking inland from the sea at the misty grey hills of the Highlands of Scotland, and the stark chunky shape of Castle Keep, set on its small rocky island. He could hear the whine of the wind, and the lapping of the waves; he could smell the sea. He heard a strange honking bark, and from other rocks closer by he saw a big dark seal heave itself up and slide down into the waves.

Emily saw the seal too; she felt that it had turned to look at her, and that for an instant she was staring into its wide black eyes. She was facing a small computer screen and yet she felt she was surrounded by the ancient mountains and the beckoning sea. She wanted passionately to be back in Scotland; it was calling her, tugging at her. She saw the same longing on Jessup's face, and she heard a quiet sigh even from Barry, who had never been there at all.

Castle Keep loomed before them across the grey-blue waves, and yet never seemed to grow closer. If they were in a boat, it was not moving, but waiting.

They heard a voice, faraway but clear, a husky, dusty, creaky voice that seemed not to have been used for a very long time, and yet filled the room around them.

'*Tha mi 'g iarraidh 'dol do'm dhuthaich fhein,*' it said, softly, plaintive as a small child. '*Tha mi 'g iarraidh 'dol do'm dhuthaich fhein.*'

Emily whispered, 'It's the Boggart! That's the piece of Gaelic that Willie read to us. '*I want to go to my own country.*'

Barry shook his head, tossing the long hair, as if to free himself from a spell. He said firmly, 'That's coming from the computer, Em.'

Jessup said quietly, 'There's no voice synthesizer in our game. That's the Boggart talking.'

'My God,' Barry said.

The husky voice spoke again, this time in a faltering, uncertain English. 'I want to go to my own country,' it said. 'My own country . . .' Then it faded into the wash of the waves, and the sighing of the wind.

The screen was dark again, filled with the black space and prickling stars of the Black Hole game; peaceful, unmoving, silent. Barry sat staring at it. He said, 'And our game is a space game. But those hills . . . and the sea, with the waves breaking . . . and that tower was, like, so real . . .'

'That's Castle Keep,' Emily said. 'That's where he lives. That's where he wants to go.'

Jessup said, wondering, 'He's amazing. He knew he couldn't talk to us on his own, so he used the computer, he used the black hole. And maybe that's the way he wants to go back.'

'Through the computer?' Barry said slowly.

'Through a Scottish computer,' Jessup said. He nudged Barry out of the chair and sat down in front of the computer. 'Tommy Cameron doesn't have one, but his father does. So what we do is, we copy the game on to a disc, and we send it to Tommy.' He reached for a box on his desk.

Barry said, 'Why don't we just email it?'

'And let the Boggart into the internet?' Jessup said. 'Are you joking?' He found a little disc in the box, and plugged it into his computer. 'When Tommy gets this, he plays it through over there, and the Boggart will know he's at home – and he'll come out of the computer and go to Castle Keep.'

Emily said uncertainly, 'How will he know he's back?'

'He just will. Like birds knowing where to go when they migrate. The Boggart may not be able to fly over the ocean, but I bet you he'll know when he's on the other side.'

Emily was trying to see Scotland in her head. 'Tommy should take his computer over to the castle, and put the disc in it there.'

'It's not a laptop – and there's no electricity in the castle, remember? His own house will do.'

Barry said, 'Is this Tommy reliable?'

'Of course he is!' Emily said indignantly.

Jessup grinned, and began the process of

copying material from the inside of the computer to the disc.

'Wait a moment,' Barry said. 'You can't copy it. You have to transfer it, lock, stock and barrel.'

Jessup stopped, horrified. He heard wild shrieks of protest inside his cautious computer-trained mind. '*Transfer* it? But then that's all there'd be, this one little disc! It could get damaged, it could get lost. You should always keep a copy of *everything*!'

'You can't copy a person,' Barry said.

Jessup paused. 'Oh,' he said. 'Yes.'

'The Boggart's inside this game. He put himself in, and he'll take himself out, I guess. But there's only one of him. You'll just have to take a risk on him.' Barry gave a small wry grin. 'That's the way it is with people,' he said.

'Here he goes, then,' Jessup said.

He took a deep breath, and his fingers spoke to the keyboard for a nerve-wracking few minutes. Then he ejected the disc and held it out. They all gazed at it, trying to absorb the idea that this small piece of metal and plastic contained all the ancient magic and mischief that was the Boggart.

'He's really in there?' Emily said, awed.

'If he's anywhere,' said Barry.

'Wait a minute,' Emily said. She put one finger gently on the little disc that lay on Jessup's palm. 'Boggart,' she said, 'we'll come back some day. We will. Our great-grandmother was a MacDevon. We'll come back to Castle Keep.'

Jessup said, 'He can't understand unless you speak Gaelic.'

'Oh yes, he can,' Emily said.

Downstairs, a voice rose; it sounded angry. They all jumped. Barry said, 'What time is it?'

Jessup peered at his clock radio. 'Seven-thirty.'

Barry groaned. 'I should have gotten out before your Mom woke up.' He looked back at the disc in Jessup's hand. '*Well, see, Mrs Volnik, I spent the night in your kid's room because he was looking for this, like, magic creature in his computer . . .*'

The voice rose higher; it was recognizable now as Maggie's voice. They heard Robert rumbling in reply, then Maggie bursting out again. To their alarm they heard her voice growing closer; she was coming up the stairs.

'Emily!' She was in the other bedroom, which was of course empty. Jessup jumped up, and Barry sat down at the desk. Emily stood in front of him.

'Emily! Have you or Jessup spoken to any reporters?' She was talking as she came through the door, wearing her dressing gown, waving a copy of the morning newspaper and trying to read it at the same time, so that she scarcely glanced at them.

'No,' Emily said. 'There was a television lady, but I hung up on her.'

'Look at this! That wretched man!' Maggie held the newspaper still long enough for them to see the headline GHOSTS IN THE ANNEXE, and underneath it a two-column story with two photographs. One showed a front view of their own house, and the other was a head-and-shoulders portrait of a solemn Dr Stigmore with his hair combed flat. He looked a little like Adolf Hitler, without the moustache.

'What is it?' Jessup said.

'Rubbish. All about how there's a poltergeist throwing furniture around this house and your father's theatre, and how the celebrated scholar of parapsychology Dr William Stigmore is thoroughly researching the circumstances.'

'Meaning me,' said Emily unhappily.

'Meaning you. And how all his findings will be revealed next week in that "Beyond Belief" TV programme, which just happens, of course, to be on the channel owned by the owner of this newspaper.' Maggie's voice rose to something like a howl. 'I will *kill* William Stigmore!'

'He's a creep,' Jessup said simply. 'He always was.'

Maggie wasn't listening. She was beginning to sound extremely English, as she always did when upset. 'If he thinks I'm going to let him do his bloody research on my daughter, he's got another think coming! How *dare* he talk about us in public, the rotten publicity hound! He's never coming near this family again – I don't care how many chairs get thrown about!'

Emily said, 'I don't think there'll be any more.'

But Maggie had caught sight of Barry. She stared at him, her hand going instinctively to push back the long hair loose about her face. 'What are you doing here?'

'Working,' Barry said.

'That makes a change,' Maggie said tartly.

Barry flushed. He opened his mouth to retaliate, and then changed his mind. 'It does, doesn't it?' he said.

Emily was about to start loathing her mother when Maggie did one of the quick engaging mood changes for which she was famous in the family. 'I'm sorry, Barry, that was a bitchy thing to say.

I'll find better ways of nagging you to finish school. You seem to have worked a miraculous cure on my son, at any rate.'

They all looked at Jessup, fully clothed, bright-eyed, the picture of health. He had forgotten he was supposed to have the flu. He looked down modestly, and his hand closed over the little computer disc.

'Let's all go have breakfast, and drink bad health to Dr Stigmore,' Maggie said.

'In just a moment,' Emily said. 'Jess and I have a quick letter to write.'

CHAPTER FOURTEEN

IT WAS a Saturday morning in Port Appin, four days after Christmas, and Tommy Cameron was helping his father Angus load boxes into his car. Angus had found no newspaper stories for several weeks, so he was at home working in the shop, and Tommy's mother was looking much happier. Business was brisk, and they had even sold nineteen of the six-dozen boxes of Christmas crackers Angus had insisted on buying secondhand in a fire sale. Tommy was as glad to see the car as he was to see his father. Making special delivery runs on a bicycle in December was a chilly business.

There was a fine mist of rain in the air, and clouds hung ragged and low over the hills and the islands. But seagulls were weaving endlessly to and fro over the sea, calling, calling. Tommy looked up at them curiously, wondering what could be making them so restless on a dank winter day.

Another sound came from the direction of the road, the growing raucous rattle of an engine in trouble, and around the corner came the bright familiar van of the postman. It was travelling in a series of strange jerky hiccups, coughing and spluttering alarmingly.

'Lord!' said Tommy's father, straightening up, peering. 'What does David Ross have in his petrol tank today, do you suppose?'

The van zigzagged towards them, and stopped with a final violent tremor and cough. The postman got out; he was a portly man with a neat grey beard. 'New Year!' he said bitterly. 'It has to choose New Year to die on me!' He glared at his van, and kicked its rear tyre.

'Poor thing,' said Angus Cameron. 'You should be kinder, David – we are all getting older.'

'This van is only two years old and it had a check-up last week,' said David Ross the postman. He opened the rear doors and began pulling parcels out of a postbag. 'The Post Office is having some sort of epidemic, if you ask me. Last night's mail train from Glasgow nearly crashed, with some sort of brake failure – and last week one of the transatlantic planes came in on one engine –'

'Dangerous occupation, postal delivery,' Angus said solemnly. 'You should take up hang gliding.'

'A happy New Year to you too,' said David Ross dourly. He handed over several boxes and a package of mail, then reached back into his bag. 'Oh, and there is a registered piece for Tommy here. A late Christmas present, I dare say.'

He pulled out a brown padded envelope – and staggered suddenly, juggling the envelope between his two hands as if it were all at once very hot, or very heavy. He handed it hastily to Tommy, who took it warily but was surprised to find it very light.

'Sign here,' David Ross said. Tommy signed his name.

'Maybe you should take my bike, Mr Ross,' he said cheerfully.

'It's been getting worse and worse all day,' the postman said morosely. He climbed back into his van and raised a resigned hand in farewell. Then he turned the ignition key.

And the engine purred into life as quietly as a kitten, and David Ross' astonished face disappeared with his van, driving smooth as silk away down the road.

Susan Cooper

'Registered, eh?' said Angus. 'Who's it from?'

Tommy looked at the stamps on his package, and the warnings printed all over it in careful capital letters:

FRAGILE ... URGENT ... HANDLE WITH CARE ...

'It's from Canada,' he said.

Dear Tommy, said the letter, when finally, privately, he opened it.

Be very VERY *careful with this disc because the Boggart has put himself inside it. It was the only way he could find to get to talk to us, and to have himself sent home. There isn't time to explain it all right now, we will write to you later.*

When you are absolutely sure there is nobody else around, read the instruction bit of this letter and put the disc in your dad's computer. There is a space game on it called Black Hole. Go into this, and follow the instructions to begin space travel.

Once you are in space, IGNORE *all the warnings on the screen that try to keep you from being swallowed up by the Black Hole. You* HAVE *to be swallowed up by the Black Hole, because the Boggart will be waiting for you on the other side of it. It is very scary having to do what the Boggart wants and not what the computer wants, but it is the only way.* YOU JUST HAVE TO FLY. TRUST US.

Once you reach the Boggart, we think he will take over, and go home to the castle. He is a pain but we will miss him. A lot.

Thanks for helping.

Merry Christmas and Happy New Year.

Jessup and Emily

PS We miss you too.

Love,

Emily

The letter had one final page after this, headed 'Instructions for Black Hole Game'.

Sitting up in bed, Tommy took a deep breath, and let it out in a long soundless whistle. He looked at the small disc lying beside him on the quilt. The Boggart had always roamed so free, here in Port Appin, in his own small world. Life must have become terribly complicated for him over there, if the only way he could find to escape was by locking himself up.

He listened to the sounds of his parents preparing for bed, in the room next door. In this small house, there was no chance of running the computer undetected at night. But he knew what he would do. Tomorrow night there would be a *ceilidh* at the village hall, a splendid communal party at which everyone would perform and sing and dance, eat and drink, and generally enjoy being together. Tommy would be part of it; unknown to Jessup and Emily, he was one of the best Scottish dancers Appin had ever produced, and he was to do a sword dance from the Isle of Skye. But after that, when the dancing had become general and his parents were laughing and talking with their friends, he knew he could slip away.

He picked up the disc and slid it under his pillow, and lay down. Before he turned out the light, he reached for the letter. He re-read the postscript, several times. Then he pushed the letter under his pillow too.

Light and music and laughter poured out of the windows and door of the village hall, with the rhythm of dancing feet and furious fiddle playing. At one moment Tommy was standing at the door, smiling, applauding, resplendent in his kilt and velvet jacket; at the next he had backed quietly away and disappeared into the night. Nobody noticed him go. He ran down the dark road, grateful that he didn't have to worry about bumping into the new owner of Castle Keep. Mr Maconochie had left the *ceilidh* early, with his two small visiting great-nephews. The little boys had had a fine time, but one of them had already fallen asleep and the other was well on the way.

Like the Volniks, Mr Maconochie the lawyer had fallen in love with Castle Keep; unlike them, he had decided to change his life and move there. Perhaps he had been waiting for an excuse to start again. For that was what he had done: he had sold his house in Edinburgh, bought all the MacDevon's remaining books and furniture from Maggie and Robert, and, just last week, sent them a large cheque that made him the new master of Castle Keep. To the great relief of the Camerons and the rest of Port Appin, his intention seemed to be to change the castle only in ways that made it safer.

Tommy sat down at his father's desk, spread out the letter of instruction, put the disc in the computer and launched himself into Jessup's Black Hole game. Soon the screen took him into space, among the glittering stars. He found that his fingers were trembling. He could feel his heart beating faster too, faster than it had beaten after his sword dance, or even before it, when he had been nervous.

Looking up at the windows, he realized that he had forgotten to draw the curtains, so he switched off the desk lamp. Now the only light in the room was that from the glimmering computer screen – and, beyond it, from the few faintly glowing windows of Castle Keep. With his great-nephews staying, Mr Maconochie kept night lights on all night long, in case they should wake up and feel lonely or alarmed.

Tommy looked back at the screen, and it drew him into the feeling of flying in a spaceship, deeper and deeper, out among the stars. The game carried him on, far into space. Like Emily and Jessup he travelled through galaxies, billions of light years in seconds, until like them he began to see the perilous quivering of the stars, and the warnings thrown up at him by the computer game. Slowly he went on, and on, nervous all the time that his inexperience with the computer would lead him to make some terrible mistake.

Suddenly the screen was full of huge glaring words.

DANGER!!!
DANGER!!!
DANGER!!!

In a hasty, frightened reflex Tommy pushed the keys that would interrupt the course of any program in the computer. He must have made some dreadful mistake. If he could stop the game, he could re-read the instructions to find out where he had gone wrong.

But to his horror, the computer ignored him. It was too late to stop.

Image after image whirled by on the screen, warning after warning. The spaceship of his imagination flew on, undeterred. Tommy could feel himself rushing through space as if it were really happening, and he fought to keep himself out of the illusion. In panic he stabbed at the keyboard, desperately trying to find some way to obey the computer and avert disaster. What had he done wrong? He was going to kill the Boggart!

Then looking wildly around, he caught sight of the words in Emily's sprawling black capitals on one of the pages beside him.

YOU JUST HAVE TO FLY. TRUST US.

The words filled Tommy's mind, pulling him out of panic, and with a sound like a sob he forced his hands away from the computer keyboard. He felt himself let go, give up control. And he was staring wide-eyed at the screen, reaching his arms wide as if for balance, as the terrifying whirlpool of the Black Hole pulled him down into the dark, down, down, into unending deathly emptiness . . .

The screen was black, quite black, save for one point of blazing blue light in the centre. Giddy, breathless, Tommy stared at it.

The blue light bounced a little, as if it were dancing. And very gradually, Tommy began to feel all the tension being drawn out of him. His mind and his body began to relax, free now from anxiety. He seemed to hear the sound of this relaxation too, warm, comforting, filling the room – and he laughed aloud as he realized it was exactly like the purring of a cat. A sense of laughter was all around him; he was at the centre of the Boggart's happiness. He stood up, wondering, and the purring sound enveloped him like music.

All at once the computer made a noise like a gunshot, and it spat out the disc in an explosion of blue flame. Tommy jumped back. The disc lay on the carpet, burning and yet cold, flickering without smell or sound. Against his face he felt for an instant a cool brief touch, as if a small hand had stroked his cheek.

He stood very still, holding his breath.

Then he heard another sudden crash, and he spun round and saw that a pane of one of the windows had shattered. And through the window, out over the dark water, he saw a blue flame flying like an arrow, through the clear night, curving out, until it touched the roof of Castle Keep, leaped up for an instant as if in triumph, and disappeared.

Tommy stood looking out, in the formal Scottish kilt and shirt and jacket of the sword dancer, and he smiled. 'Do *bheatha dhachaidh*, Boggart,' he said. 'Welcome home.'

In a gentle whirl of sooty dust the Boggart dropped down the chimney and out into the broad living-room hearth of Castle Keep. He breathed a long happy sigh. Then he put himself through the gap under the door and flittered into the kitchen, which seemed warmer than he remembered, and he twitched at the tail of a prowling mouse. The mouse squeaked indignantly, and the Boggart saw fragments of sandwiches lying on the table near two small plates, as if two small people had left the remnants of a snack. He popped a piece into his mouth, and tasted peanut butter. He smiled.

In the glow of the night lights he flittered happily round the castle, greeting every stone and board and corner, every room and door. Nothing had changed. It was all the same as before, though cleaner. He drifted into the MacDevon's bedroom, and found the wardrobe full of clothes that were not the MacDevon's but similar, and in the MacDevon's bed a sleeping man who breathed with the same right kind of gentle snore. The Boggart beamed a welcome, and tied Mr Maconochie's shoelaces together to greet him in the morning.

In the next room, to his delight, he found two small sleeping boys, of a perfect age for Boggart teasings, and he flittered busily about the house until he found a needle and thread. Then he came back and sewed neat little stitches across the ends of the sleeves of one boy's shirt, and the legs of the other one's jeans. He would take care to be hovering, appreciative and invisible when they woke up and began to dress.

In a sheltered corner downstairs he heard a sleeping dog whimper at his passing, and when he went to investigate he found not an experienced adult dog or a tired half-blind wreck, but a big-pawed, flop-eared Labrador puppy. The Boggart could hardly believe his luck. Here was someone else with whom he could have great fun. As a beginning, he caught a large black beetle and dropped it in the puppy's water bowl.

In the sleeping castle, the Boggart paused at one of the narrow outer windows that opened towards the Island of Mull. Tomorrow he would visit the seals, on the rocks out there. A picture flickered through his wild mind, of two boys and a girl, whom he had watched visiting the seals once, but he could not remember their names.

He looked out at the glimmering sea and the islands, and the sky lit with stars that had seen all the great or terrible things that had ever happened in Scotland, through more years even than a boggart. Echoing faintly over the water from the village hall, he heard the joyful skirl of a single bagpipe. Then he flittered away to the library, and found that his own special place was still there, the space between two blocks of stone high in the library wall, where three hundred years earlier an absent-minded mason had forgotten to put mortar, and an absent-minded carpenter had hidden the forgetfulness with a shelf. The Boggart curled up, contented, at home, and went to sleep.

ABOUT THE AUTHOR

SUSAN COOPER

1935	Born 23 May in Burnham in Buckinghamshire, England
1945	Goes to Slough High School, a local grammar school
1953	Attends Somerville College, University of Oxford where she studies English. Becomes the first female editor of the university newspaper, Cherwell.
1956	Graduates from Oxford with an MA degree in English
1957–63	Works as a journalist and feature writer for the Sunday Times and writes in her spare time. Begins work on The Dark Is Rising series.

1963   *Marries and moves to the USA, where she has two children. Becomes a full-time writer.*

1964   Mandrake, *her debut science fiction novel for adults, is published by Hodder & Stoughton*

1965   Over Sea, Under Stone – *the first book in the children's fantasy sequence* The Dark Is Rising – *is published*

1970   Dawn of Fear, *a novel about her experiences during the Second World War, is published*

1973   The Dark Is Rising, *the second book in the sequence, wins a Newbery Honor as a runner-up for the Newbery Medal, one of America's most prestigious prizes for children's literature. Spends the next six years writing the rest of the sequence:* Greenwitch, The Grey King *and* Silver on the Tree.

1976   The Grey King *wins the Newbery Medal, and the inaugural Tir na n-Og Award for English language books with a Welsh setting*

1977   Silver on the Tree *wins the Tir na n-Og Award*

1983   Seaward *is published and receives the Janusz Korczak Literary Prize, an international award for books promoting friendship and understanding*

1993   The Boggart *is published and is shortlisted for the 1993 Smarties Award and the 1994 Carnegie Medal, one of the most prestigious children's book awards in the UK*

1997	*Its sequel,* The Boggart and the Monster, *is published and wins one of the Scottish Arts Council's first Children's Book Awards*
1999	King of Shadows *is published and is shortlisted for the Carnegie Medal*
2002	*Is the US nominee for the Hans Christian Andersen Award for lasting contribution to children's literature.* Green Boy *is published.*
2006	Victory *is published*
2012	*Wins the lifetime Margaret A. Edwards Award from the American Library Association for her contribution to writing for young people*
2013	Ghost Hawk *is published and is shortlisted for the Carnegie Medal*
2018	*A new Boggart adventure,* The Boggart Fights Back, *is published*

INTERESTING FACTS

In British folklore, boggarts are usually attached to houses and to particular people – they can bring good luck if they're treated well. If a boggart's human family moves house, then the boggart will often follow them.

Port Appin is a real fishing village in the west of Scotland. Just over a mile up the coast is an island with a fourteenth-century castle on it – Castle Stalker (the inspiration for the Boggart's Castle Keep).

WHERE DID THE
STORY COME FROM?

Susan Cooper says:

*My bookshelves have always been full of English, Welsh,
Scottish and Irish folktales, many of which overlap with
each other, and for a while I wrote picture books based on
some of them with the artist Warwick Hutton:* The Silver
Cow, The Selkie Girl, Tam Lin. *I always wanted to invent
a story about a boggart, the shape-shifting character in
tales from Scotland and the North of England, but I could
never decide where to start. Then one day I was on
holiday in Scotland with my best friend, Zoe, driving
along the coast of a loch, when we turned a corner and
suddenly I saw a magical small castle, alone on an island
in the water. Zoe said afterwards, 'You were quiet for such
a long time after we saw the castle.' I'd been listening to a
happy little voice inside my head, saying to me, 'That's
where the Boggart lives!'*

GUESS WHO?

A A very ancient, mischievous thing, solitary and sly, born of a magic as old as the rocks and the waves.

B [. . .] lean and graceful and slightly taller than her husband, especially when wearing high heels.

C A tall thin man with a lot of dark hair [. . .] He wore a charcoal-grey business suit, very well cut, and a tie.

D [. . .] curly black hair and a sunburned nose, and very blue eyes.

E She was a short, precise woman, wearing an apron that was clearly newly ironed. Like her shop, she looked ferociously clean.

ANSWERS: A) The Boggart B) Maggie C) Dr Stigmore D) Tommy E) Mrs Cameron

WORDS GLORIOUS WORDS!

We often come across **new** or **unfamiliar** words when we're reading. Here are a few unusual words you'll find in this Puffin book. Did you spot any others?

coracle *a small wicker boat that's often covered in a waterproof layer of animal skin or tar*

electrode *the name for an electrical conductor, usually a small piece of metal, that takes electricity to or from a power source*

gobo *a stencil or template placed in front of a theatrical light to control the shape of its beam*

parapsychology *the study of mental skills that go beyond the known laws of nature or science, such as seeing into the future or moving objects without touching them*

poltergeist *a mischievous and sometimes disruptive ghost or spirit*

psychokinesis *the ability to move objects using only the power of the mind and without physically touching them*

pwca *pronounced 'poo-ka' – a Welsh version of a boggart*

ululation *a howling or wailing sound*

vigil *the act of staying awake, often throughout the night, to keep watch over something or someone*

A GUIDE TO SCOTTISH GAELIC

There are two families of Celtic languages. One includes Scottish Gaelic, Irish Gaelic and the extinct language of the Isle of Man, all closely related. The other includes Welsh, Cornish and Breton, which are also closely related but quite unlike the Gaelic. Here are some Scottish Gaelic words you may have spotted in The Boggart.

Rèilig Odhrain [Pronounced: ray'lig oh'rine] *An ancient cemetery on the Isle of Iona*

Samhain [Pronounced: SAH-win] *An ancient Celtic festival to mark the beginning of winter, celebrated on the first day of November*

Cailleach Bheur [Pronounced: cal'yach vare] *The blue-faced hag of winter*

Tha mi 'giaraidh 'dol do'm dhuthiach fhein [Pronounced: ha mee gee-ur-ree dol dom ghoo-eekh hayn] *In English this means 'I want to go to my own country'*

ceilidh [Pronounced: kay-li] *The Gaelic word for a gathering, which usually involves music and dancing*

Do bheatha dhachaidh [Pronounced: duh vah'uh ghah'khee] *'Welcome home' in Gaelic*

QUIZ

Thinking caps on – let's see how much you can remember! Answers are at the bottom of the next page.

1 What is the name of the loch that surrounds Castle Keep?

a) *Loch Ness*

b) *Loch Lomond*

c) *Loch Linnhe*

d) *Loch Morar*

2 What are the two sweet sauces that the Boggart discovers, and enjoys, in Canada?

a) *Apple sauce and maple syrup*

b) *Fudge sauce and apple sauce*

c) *Fudge sauce and chocolate sauce*

d) *Caramel sauce and fudge sauce*

3 *What do Emily and Jessup dress up as for Halloween?*

a) *Emily is a ghost and Jessup is the Boggart*

b) *Emily is a vampire and Jessup is a spider*

c) *Emily is a vampire and Jessup is Ice Death*

d) *Emily is a witch and Jessup is a ghoul*

4 *How does Barry get to Jessup's house in the blizzard?*

a) *In a taxi*

b) *On skis*

c) *On a bike*

d) *By train*

5 *How does the Boggart get home to Scotland?*

a) *In a suitcase*

b) *In a desk*

c) *In a vase*

d) *In a computer disc*

ANSWERS: 1) c 2) b 3) c 4) b 5) d

IN
THIS YEAR

1993
Fact Pack

*What else was
happening in the
world when this book
was first published?*

The Queen announces that **Buckingham Palace**
will open its doors to the public for the first time.

From April to October, the **Mississippi** and **Missouri
Rivers** flood large portions of the American Midwest.

The big films of the year are **Jurassic Park** and **Mrs
Doubtfire**.

There is a major **ecological catastrophe** when an
oil-tanker runs aground near the Shetland Islands, resulting
in 84,700 tonnes of crude oil being spilled into the North Sea.

MAKE
AND
DO

Make an
ice-cream
sundae!

The Boggart loves vanilla ice cream and fudge sauce.
Follow this easy recipe to make a delicious treat using
your own favourite ice cream flavours.

YOU WILL NEED:

* 3 tubs of different-flavoured ice cream (e.g. vanilla, chocolate and strawberry)

* One or two bottles of sweet sauce, such as strawberry, chocolate or fudge

* Sprinkles, sweets and berries to decorate your sundae

* Bowls or sundae glasses to serve

Place three scoops of your favourite ice creams into a bowl.

 Drizzle some sauce over each scoop – you could stick to one flavour or try several!

 Decorate your sundae with sprinkles, sweets or pieces of fruit.

 TUCK IN – before the Boggart has a chance to!

DID YOU KNOW?

James I of England *(James VI of Scotland) wrote a number of books, including* Daemonologie *and* A Counterblaste Against Tobacco, *which are mentioned in* The Boggart. *But he's best remembered for a book that he didn't write. In 1604, he ordered a new translation of* the Bible *into English. Today, this translation remains one of the most important and influential books in the English-speaking world.*

In Scottish folklore, the Cailleach Bheur *is a hag who personifies winter, the daughter of the winter sun. She is said to spend each summer as a standing stone, waking up on Halloween.*

Different sorts of boggart appear in several other fantasy series, such as the Chronicles of Narnia *by C. S. Lewis and J. K. Rowling's* Harry Potter *books.*

PUFFIN
WRITING
TIPS

Imagine how your morning routine would be different if you had magical powers!

Write a description of your hometown – as if you were talking to an alien.

Keep a travel journal when you go on holiday so you can capture all the exciting new sights and sounds.